Limerick County Library

D0272914

THE UNFINISHED
NOVEL *and*
OTHER STORIES

ALSO BY VALERIE MARTIN

Salvation: Scenes from the Life of St Francis
Property
Italian Fever
The Great Divorce
Mary Reilly
The Consolation of Nature: Short Stories
A Recent Martyr
Alexandra
Set in Motion
Love: Short Stories

THE UNFINISHED NOVEL *and* OTHER STORIES

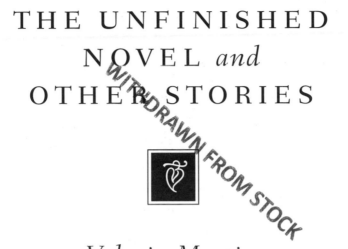

Valerie Martin

LIMERICK
COUNTY LIBRARY
00502829

Weidenfeld & Nicolson

LONDON

First published in Great Britain in 2006
by Weidenfeld & Nicolson

1 3 5 7 9 10 8 6 4 2

© Valerie Martin 2006

Some of the stories first appeared in US publications:
His Blue Period (*Ploughshares*, 1998); The Open Door
(*Massachusetts Review*, 2002); The Change (*Ploughshares*, 1998).

All characters in this publication are fictitious and
any resemblance to real persons,
living or dead, is purely coincidental.

All rights reserved. No part of this publication may be
reproduced, stored in a retrieval system, or transmitted,
in any form or by any means, electronic, mechanical,
photocopying, recording or otherwise, without the prior
permission of both the copyright owner and the above publisher.

The right of Valerie Martin to be identified as the
author of this work has been asserted in accordance
with the Copyright, Designs and Patents Act 1988.

A CIP catalogue record for this book
is available from the British Library.

ISBN- 97 8 02978 4855 4
ISBN- 0 297 84855 0

Typeset at The Spartan Press Ltd,
Lymington, Hants

Printed in Great Britain by
Clays Ltd, St Ives plc

Weidenfeld & Nicolson

The Orion Publishing Group Ltd
Orion House
5 Upper Saint Martin's Lane
London, WC2H 9EA

The Orion publishing group's policy is to use papers that
are natural, renewable and recyclable products and made
from wood grown in sustainable forests. The logging and
manufacturing processes are expected to conform to the
environmental regulations of the country of origin.

www.orionbooks.co.uk

For Dr. Martin and Counselor Hayes

CONTENTS

HIS BLUE PERIOD

For anyone who has met Meyer Anspach since his success, his occasional lyrical outbursts on the subject of his blue period may be merely tedious, but for those of us who actually remember the ceaseless whine of paranoia that constituted his utterances at that time, Anspach's rhapsodies on the character-building properties of poverty are infuriating. Most of what he says about those days is sheer fabrication, but two things are true: He was poor—we all were—and he was painting all the time. He never mentions, perhaps he doesn't know, a detail I find most salient, which is that his painting actually was better then than it is now. Like so many famous artists, these days Anspach does an excellent imitation of Anspach. He's in control, nothing slips by him, he has spent the last twenty years attending to Anspach's painting and he has no desire ever to attend to anything else. But when he was young, when he was with Maria, no one, including Anspach, had any idea what an Anspach was. He was brash, intense, never satisfied, feeling his way into a wilderness. He had no character to speak of, or rather he had already the character he has now, which is entirely self-absorbed and egotistical. He cared for no one, certainly not for Maria, though he liked to proclaim that he could not live without her, that she was his inspiration, his muse, that she was absolutely essential to his life as an artist.

Pursuing every other woman who caught his attention was also essential, and making no effort to conceal those often sleazy and heartless affairs, was, well, part of his character.

If struggle, poverty and rejection actually did build character, Maria should have been an Everest in the mountain range of character, unassailable, white-peaked, towering above us in the unbreathably thin air. But of course she wasn't. She was devoted to Anspach and so she never stopped weeping. She wept for years. Often she appeared at the door of my studio tucking her sodden handkerchief into her skirt pocket, smoothing back the thick, damp strands of her remarkable black hair, a carrot clutched in her small, white fist. I knew she was there even if I had my back to her because the rabbits came clattering out from wherever they were sleeping and made a dash for the door. Then I would turn and see her kneeling on the floor with the two rabbits pressing against her, patting her skirt with their delicate paws and lifting their soft, twitching muzzles to her hands to encourage her tender caresses, which they appeared to enjoy as much as the carrot they knew was coming their way. My rabbits were wild about Maria. Later, when we sat at the old metal table drinking coffee, the rabbits curled up at her feet, and later still, when she got up to make her way back to Anspach, they followed her to the door and I had to herd them back into the studio after she was gone.

I was in love with Maria and we all knew it. Anspach treated it as a joke, he was that sure of himself. There could be no serious rival to a genius such as his, and no woman in her right mind would choose warmth, companionship, affection and support over service at the high altar of Anspach. Maria tried not to encourage me, but she was so beaten down, so starved for a kind word, that occasionally she couldn't resist a few moments of rest. On weekends we worked together at a popular restaurant on

Spring Street, so we rode the train together, over and back. Sometimes, coming home just before dawn on the D train, when the cars came out of the black tunnel and climbed slowly up into the pale blush of morning light over the East River, Maria went so far as to lean her weary head against my arm. I didn't have the heart, or was it the courage, ever to say the words that rattled in my brain, repeated over and over in time to the metallic clanking of the wheels, "Leave him, come to me." Maria, I judged, perhaps wrongly, didn't need her life complicated by another artist who couldn't make a living.

I had the restaurant job, which paid almost nothing, though the tips were good, and one day a week I built stretchers for an art supply house near the Bowery, where I was paid in canvas and paint. That was it. But I lived so frugally I was able to pay the rent and keep myself and the rabbits in vegetables, which was what we ate. Maria had another job, two nights a week at a Greek restaurant on Atlantic Ave. Because she worked at night she usually slept late; so did Anspach. When they got up, she cooked him a big meal, did the shopping, housekeeping, bill paying, enthused over his latest production and listened to his latest tirade about the art establishment. In the afternoon Anspach went out for an espresso, followed by a trip downtown to various galleries where he berated the owners, if he could get near them, or the hired help, if he couldn't. Anspach said painting was his vocation, this carping at the galleries was his business, and he was probably right. In my romantic view of myself as an artist, contact with the commercial world was humiliating and demeaning; I couldn't bear to do it in the flesh. I contented myself with sending out pages of slides every few months, then, when they came back, adding a few new ones, switching them around, and sending them out again.

On those afternoons when Anspach was advancing his career, Maria came to visit me. We drank coffee, talked, smoked cigarettes. Sometimes I took out a pad and did quick sketches of her, drowsy over her cigarette, the rabbits dozing at her feet. I listened to her soft voice, looked into her dark eyes and tried to hold up my end of the conversation without betraying the sore and aching state of my heart. We were both readers, though where Maria found time to read I don't know. We talked about books. We liked cheerful, optimistic authors: Kafka, Céline, Beckett. Maria introduced me to their lighthearted predecessors, Hardy and Gissing. Her favorite novel was *Jude the Obscure*.

She had come to the city when she was seventeen with the idea that she would become a dancer. She spent six years burying this dream beneath a mountain of rejection, though she did once get as close as the classrooms of the ABT. At last she concluded that it was not her will or even her ability that held her back, it was her body. She wasn't tall enough and her breasts were too large. She had begun to accept this as the simple fact it was when she met Anspach and dancing became not her ambition but her refuge. She continued to attend classes a few times a week. The scratchy recordings of Chopin, the polished wooden floors, the heft of the bar, the sharp jabs and rebukes of the martinet teachers, the cunning little wooden blocks that disfigured her toes, the smooth, tight skin of the leotard, the strains, pains, the sweat, all of it was restorative to Maria; it was the reliable world of routine, secure and predictable, as different from the never-ending uproar of life with Anspach as a warm bath is from a plunge into an ice storm at sea.

Anspach had special names for everyone, always designed to be mildly insulting. He called Maria, Mah-ree, or Miss Poppin-cockulous, a perversion of her real surname, which was Greek.

Fidel, the owner of a gallery Anspach browbeat into showing his paintings, was "Fido." Paul, an abstract painter, who counted himself among Anspach's associates, was "Pile." My name is John, but Anspach always called me Jack; he still does. He says it with a sharp punch to it, as if it is part of a formula, like, "Watch out, Jack," or, "You won't get Jack if you keep that up." Even my rabbits were not rabbits to Anspach, but "Jack's-bun-buns," pronounced as one word with the stress on the last syllable. If he returned from the city before Maria got home, he came straight to my studio and launched into a long, snide monologue, oily with sexual insinuation, on the subject of how hard it was to be a poor artist who couldn't keep his woman at home because whenever he went out to attend to his business she was sure to sneak away to visit jacksbunbuns, and he didn't know what was so appealing about those bunbuns, but his Miss Poppincockulous just couldn't seem to get enough of them. That was the way Anspach talked. Maria didn't try to defend herself and I was no help. I generally offered Anspach a beer, which he never refused, and tried to change the subject to the only one I knew he couldn't resist, the state of his career. Then he sat down at the table and indulged himself in a flood of vitriol against whatever galleries he'd been in that day. His most frequent complaint was that they were all looking for pictures to hang "over the couch," in the awful living rooms of "Long Island Jane and Joe," or "Fire Island Joe and Joey." He pronounced Joey, "jo-EE." Sometimes if he suspected I had another beer in the refrigerator, Anspach would ask to see what I was painting. Then and only then, as we stood looking at my most recent canvas, did he have anything to say worth hearing.

I don't know what he really thought of me as a painter, but given his inflated opinion of his own worth, any interest he showed in someone else was an astonishing compliment. I know he thought I was facile, but that was because he was himself a very poor draftsman, he still is, and I draw with ease. Anspach's gift was his sense of color, which, even then, was astounding. It was what ultimately made him famous: then Anspach's passion for color was all that made him bearable. It was the reason I forgave him for being Anspach.

His blue period started in the upper right-hand corner of a painting titled *Napalm*, which featured images from the Vietnam War. A deep purple silhouette of the famous photograph of a young girl fleeing her burning village was repeated around the edges like a frame. The center was a blush of scarlet, gold and black, like the inside of a poppy. In the upper corner was a mini-landscape, marsh grass, strange, exotic trees, a few birds in flight against an eerie, unearthly sky. The sky was not really blue but a rich blue-green with coppery undertones, a Renaissance color, like the sky in a painting by Bellini.

"How did you get this?" I asked, pointing at the shimmery patch of sky.

"Glazes," he said. "It took a while, but I can do it again." He gazed at the color with his upper teeth pressed into his lower lip, a speculative, anxious expression in his open, innocent eyes. Anspach fell in love with a color the way most men fall in love with a beautiful, mysterious, fascinating, unattainable woman. He gave himself over to his passion without self-pity, without vanity or envy, without hope really. It wasn't the cold spirit of rage and competitiveness which he showed for everything and every-one else in his world. It was unselfish admiration, a helpless opening of the heart. This blue-green patch, which he'd labored over patiently and lovingly, was in the background now, like a lovely, shy young woman just entering a crowded ballroom by a side door, but she had captured Anspach's imagination and it would not be long before he demanded that all the energy in the scene revolve around her and her alone.

In the weeks that followed, as that blue moved to the foreground of Anspach's pictures, it sometimes seemed to me that it was draining the life out of Maria, as if it were actually the color of her blood and Anspach had found some way to drain it directly from her veins onto his canvas.

One summer evening, after Anspach had drunk all my beers and Maria declared herself too tired and hot to cook, we treated ourselves to dinner at the Italian restaurant underneath my loft. There we ran into Paul Remy and a shy, nearsighted sculptor named Mike Brock, whom Anspach immediately christened Mac. Jack-and-Mac became the all-purpose name for Mike and myself, which Anspach used for the rest of the evening whenever he addressed one of us. After the meal Anspach invited us all to his loft to drink cheap wine and have a look at his latest work. It was Maria's night off; I could see that she was tired, but she encouraged us to come. She had, she explained, a fresh baklava from the restaurant which we should finish up as it wouldn't keep. So up we all went, grateful to pass an evening at no expense, and I, at least, was curious to see what Anspach was up to.

The loft had once been a bank building. Anspach and Maria had the whole second floor, which was wide open from front to back with long, double-sashed windows at either end. The kitchen was minimal—a small refrigerator, a two-burner stove, an old, stained sink that looked as though it should be attached to a washing machine and a low counter with a few stools gathered around it. Their bedroom was a mattress half-hidden by some curtains Maria had sewn together from the inevitable Indian bedspreads of that period. In the center of the room was a battered brick red couch, three lawn chairs and two tables made of old crates. Anspach's big easel and paint cart were in the front of the long room facing the street windows. The best thing about the place was the line of ceiling fans down the middle, left over from the bank incarnation. It was hellish outside that night, and we all sighed with relief at how much cooler the loft was than the claustrophobic tomato-laced atmosphere of the restaurant.

Maria put on a record, Brazilian music, I think, which made the seediness of the place seem less threatening, more exotic, and she poured out tumblers of wine for us all. The paintings Anspach showed us fascinated me. He was quoting bits from other painters, whom he referred to as "the Massas," but the color combinations were unexpected and everywhere there was a marvelous balance of refined technique and sheer serendipity. These days he fakes the surprise element, but his technical skill has never failed him. When Anspach talked about paint it was like a chemist talking about drugs. He knew what was in every color, what it would do in combination with other mediums, with oil, with thinner, on canvas, on pasteboard. He could give a quick run-down on all the possible side effects. Even then he didn't use much in the way of premixed colors, he made his own. His blue was underpainted with cadmium yellow, covered with a mix of phthalo green and Prussian blue and a few opalescent glazes that he called his "secret recipe." The images were recondite, personal. I was pleased to see that he was leaving the Vietnam subject matter behind with the cadmium red he'd given up in favor of the blue. The blue allowed him to be less strident, more interior. He pointed at a section of one large canvas in which a woman's hands were grasping the rim of a dark blue hole—was she pulling herself out or slipping in? The hands were carefully, lovingly painted, extraordinarily lifelike. "That," Anspach said, "is what I call painterly."

Paul turned to Maria. "Did he make you hang from the balcony?" he said, for, of course, we all knew, the hands were hers.

"Something like that," she said.

Later, when we were sitting in the lawn chairs and Maria changed the record to something vaguely Mediterranean, interrupted now and then by a high-pitched male voice screaming in agony, Anspach caught me watching her. I was looking at the long, beautiful curve of her neck—she had her hair pulled up because of the heat—and the prominent bones at the base of her throat which gleamed in the dim lamplight as if they'd been touched by one of Anspach's secret opalescent glazes.

Anspach shot me a look like a dagger. "Miss Mah-ree," he began. "Oh Miss Mah-ree, dat music is so nice. Why don't you do a little dance for us boys, Miss Mah-ree, Miss Poppincockulous, I know these boys would love to see the way you can dance, wouldn't you, Jack-and-Mac? Mr. Jack-and-Mac would especially like to see our Miss Mah-ree do a little dance to dat nice music."

Maria looked up. "Don't be silly," she said.

Anspach refilled his glass. Cheap wine brings out the worst in everyone, I thought. Then he swallowed a big mouthful and started up again, this time a little louder and with a wounded, edgy quality to his voice, like a child protesting injustice. "Oh Miss Mah-ree, don't say I'm being silly, don't say that. Don't say you won't dance for us boys, because we all want you to dance so much to dat nice music, and I know you can, Miss Mah-ree, Miss Poppincockulous, I know you like to dance for all the boys and you can take off your shirt so all the boys can see your pretty breasts, because she does have such pretty baboobies, don't you know boys, Mr. Jack-and-Mac and Mr. Pile, I know you boys would love to see Miss Mah-ree's pretty baboobies, especially you, Mr. Jack-and-Mac, Miss Mah-ree don't say no to these nice boys."

Maria sent me a guarded look, then raised her weary eyes to Anspach, who was sunk deep in the couch with his arms out over the cushions, his head dropped back, watching her closely through lowered lids. "I would never do that," she said. "I would be too shy."

Anspach made a mock smile, stretching his lips tight and flat over his teeth. "She's too shy," he said softly. Then he closed his eyes and whined, "Oh, please, Miss Mah-ree, don't be shy, oh don't be too shy, oh pleasepleasepleasepleaseplease, my Miss Mah-ree, don't be shy to dance for us boys here to that nice music, and take your shirt off, oh pleasepleasepleaseplease, I know you can, I know you're not too shy, oh pleasepleaseplease-pleaseplease."

"For God's sake, Anspach," I said. "Would you leave it alone."

Anspach addressed the ceiling. "Oh, Mr. Jack-and-Mac, look at that, he don't want to see Miss Mah-ree dance, he has no interest at all in Miss Mah-ree's pretty breasts, can you believe that? I don't believe that."

Paul groaned and set his empty glass down on one of the crates. "I've got to be going," he said. "It's late."

Anspach leaned forward, resting his elbows on his knees. "Pile has to scurry home," he said. "It's much too late for Pile."

"Yeah, me too," said Mike. "I've got to be downtown early."

I looked at Maria, who was standing with her back to the record player. She hadn't moved during Anspach's tiresome monologue. She looked pale, ghostly, her eyes were focused on empty space, and as I watched her she raised one hand and pressed her fingertips against her forehead, as if pushing back something that was trying to get out. I too maintained that I was tired, that it was late, and pulled myself out of my lawn chair while Paul and Mike, exchanging the blandest of farewell pleasantries, followed Maria to the door. I stood looking down at Anspach, who was slumped over his knees muttering something largely unintelligible, though the words "too late" were repeated at close intervals. I was disgusted and angry enough to speak my mind, and I thought of half a dozen things to say to him, but as I was sorting through them, Maria, turning from the doorway, caught my eye, and her expression so clearly entreated me to say nothing that I held my tongue and walked out past the couch to join her at the door.

"I'm sorry," she said when I was near her.

"Don't be," I said. "You didn't do anything."

"He's just drunk," she said.

I took her hands and looked into her sad face. She kept her eyes down and her body turned away, toward Anspach, back to Anspach. "You look tired," I said. "You should get some sleep."

She smiled dimly, still averting her eyes from mine, and I thought, he won't let her sleep. As I walked through the quiet streets to my studio I blamed myself for what had happened. I should not have stared at her so openly, so admiringly. But couldn't a man admire his friend's girlfriend, was that such a crime? Wouldn't any ordinary man be pleased to see his choice confirmed in his friend's eyes? Of course the fact that Anspach was not, in any meaningful sense of the word, my or anyone else's friend, gave the lie to my self-serving protest. That and the fact that what I felt for Maria was much more than admiration and I had no doubt it showed, that Anspach had seen it. He knew I wanted to take Maria away from him. He also knew I couldn't do it.

After that night I saw less and less of Maria. Sometimes she still came by in the afternoons when Anspach was in town, but she never stayed long and seemed anxious to be back in their loft before he got home. She had picked up a third, grueling, thankless job, three days a week at an art supply house in Soho. The pay was minimum wage but she got a discount on paint, which had become the lion's share of her monthly budget. Anspach was turning out paintings at an astounding rate, and the cadmium yellow that went into his blue was ten dollars a tube. The discount went to his head, and more and more paint went onto each canvas. He was cavalier about the expense, passing on his nearly empty tubes to Paul, because he couldn't be bothered to finish them. Paul had invented a special device, a kind of press, to squeeze the last dabs of color from his paint tubes.

It was about that time that I met Yvonne Remy, Paul's sister, who had come down from Vermont to study art history at NYU. She was staying with Paul until she could find a place of her own and the three of us soon fell into a routine of dinners together several nights a week, taking turns on the cooking. Yvonne was quick-witted and energetic, and she loved to talk about painting. Gradually we all noticed that she was spending more time at my place than at her brother's, and gradually we all came to feel that this was as it should be.

Yvonne was there that afternoon when I last saw Maria. She hadn't visited me in three weeks. She looked exhausted, which wasn't surprising, but there was something more than that, something worse than that, a listlessness beyond fatigue. The rabbits came running as they always did when Maria arrived, and she brightened momentarily as she bent down to caress them, but I noticed she had forgotten to bring a carrot.

Yvonne responded to her with that sudden affinity which women sometimes show each other for reasons that are inexplicable to men. She warmed the milk for the coffee, which she did not always bother with for herself, and set out some fruit, cheese and bread. When Maria showed no interest in this offering, she got up, put a few cookies on a plate and seemed relieved when Maria took one and laid it on the saucer of her cup. Maria leaned over her chair to scratch a rabbit's ears, then sat up and took a bite of the cookie. "John," she said, her eyes still on the docile creatures at her feet. "You'll always take care of these rabbits, won't you?"

"Of course," I assured her. "These rabbits and I are in this together."

When she was gone, Yvonne sat at the table idly turning her empty cup.

"She seems so tired," I said.

"She's in despair," Yvonne observed.

Then a few things happened very quickly. I didn't find out about any of it until it was all over and Maria was gone. Anspach was offered a space in a three-man show with two up-and-coming painters at the Rite Gallery. This coup, Paul told me later, with a grimace of pain at the pun, was the result of Anspach's fucking Mrs Rite on the floor of her office and suggesting to her, post-coitus, that she was the only woman in New York who could understand his work. I didn't entirely believe this story; it didn't sound like Anspach to me, but evidently it was true, for within three months Mrs Rite had left Mr Rite and Anspach was the star of her new gallery, Rivage, which was one of the first to move south into Tribeca.

Paul maintained that Anspach told Maria about his new alliance, omitting none of the details, though it is possible that she heard about it somewhere else. Mrs Rite was not bothered by the gossip, in fact, she was rumored to have been the source of much of it. As far as Anspach was concerned, he had seized an opportunity, as what self-respecting artist would not, faced with the hypocrisy and callousness of the art scene in the city. He had decided early on to enter the fray, by bombast or seduction or whatever it took, marketing himself as an artist who would not be denied.

Maria had narrowed her life to thankless drudgery and Anspach. She had given up her dance classes, she had few friends, and she had never been much given to confiding her difficulties to others. She was, as Yvonne had observed, already in despair. However she heard it, the truth about Anspach's golden opportunity was more than she could bear. Anspach told the police they'd had an argument, that she had gone out the door in a rage, that he assumed she was going to weep to one of her friends. Instead she climbed the interior fire ladder to the roof, walked across the litter of exhaust vents and peeling water pipes, pulled aside the low rickety wire mesh partition that protected the gutters and dived headfirst into the street. It was a chilly day in October; the windows were closed in the loft. Anspach didn't know what had happened until the Sicilian who owned the coffee bar on the street level rushed up the stairs and banged on his door, shouting something Anspach didn't, at first, understand.

There was no funeral in New York. Maria's father came out from Wisconsin and arranged to have her body shipped back home. It was as if she had simply disappeared. I didn't see

Anspach; I purposely avoided him. I knew if I saw him I would try to hit him. Anspach is a big man; he outweighs me by sixty pounds, I'd guess, and he's powerfully built. So I may have avoided him because I was afraid of what would happen to me.

Paul told me that a few weeks after Maria's death, Anspach moved in with Mrs Rite, and that he'd sold two of the nine paintings in the group show. At his one-man show the following year, he sold everything but the four biggest, proving his theory that the public was intent on hanging their pictures over the couch. Paul Remy saw the show and reported that Anspach's blue period was definitely over. The predominant hue was a shell pink and the repeated image was a billowing parachute. This irritated me. Everything I heard about Anspach irritated me, but I couldn't keep myself from following his career, stung with frustration, anger and envy at each new success.

In the spring, Yvonne and I moved a few blocks south, where we had more room for the same money and a small walled-in yard which soon became the rabbits' domain. They undertook amazing excavation projects, after which they spent hours cleaning their paws and sleeping in the sun, or in the shade of an ornamental beech. I kept my promise to Maria; I took good care of the rabbits for many years. They lived to be old by rabbit standards, nearly eleven, and they died within a few weeks of each other, as secretly as they could, in a den they'd dug behind the shed I'd put up for Yvonne's gardening tools and our daughter's outdoor toys. After Yvonne finished school she moved from job to job for a few years until she settled in the ceramics division at the Brooklyn Museum. I took what work I could find and kept painting. Occasionally, always through friends, I got a few pictures in a group show, but nothing sold. Storage was a continual and vexing problem. My canvases got smaller and smaller.

Paul and I were offered a joint show at a new gallery on the edge of Tribeca, an unpromising location at best. The opening was not a fashionable scene, very cheap wine, plastic cups, a few plates strewn with wedges of rubbery cheese. The meager crowd of celebrants was made up largely of the artists' friends and relatives. The artists themselves, dressed in their best jeans and T-shirts, huddled together near the back, keeping up a pointless conversation in order to avoid overhearing any chance remarks about the paintings. I was naturally surprised when there appeared above the chattering heads of this inelegant crowd the expensively coiffed, unnaturally tan and generally prosperous-looking head of Meyer Anspach.

"Slumming," Paul said to me when he spotted Anspach.

I smiled. David Hines, the gallery owner, had come to riveted attention and flashed Paul and me a look of triumph as he stepped out to welcome Anspach. Greta, a friend of Paul's who painted canvases that were too big for most gallery walls, and who was, I knew, a great admirer of Anspach's, set her plastic cup on the drinks table and rubbed her eyes hard with her knuckles.

David was ushering Anspach past the paintings, which he scarcely glanced at, to the corner where Paul and I stood open-mouthed. Anspach launched into a monologue about how we had all been poor painters together, poor artists in Brooklyn, doing our best work, because we were unknown and had only ourselves to please. This was during his blue period, a long time ago, those paintings were some of his favorites, a turning point, the suffering of that time had liberated him, he couldn't afford to buy back those paintings himself, that's how valuable they had become.

This was the first time I heard Anspach's litany about his blue period.

It was awful standing there, with David practically rubbing his hands together for glee and Paul emanating hostility, while Anspach went on and on about the brave comrade painters of long ago. Cheap wine, free love. *La Vie de Bohème*, I thought, only Maria didn't die of tuberculosis. I couldn't think of anything to say, or rather my thoughts came in such a rush I couldn't sort one out for delivery, but Paul came to my rescue by pointing out with quiet dignity that he and I still lived in Brooklyn. Then David got the idea of taking a photograph of Anspach and Anspach said he'd come to see the pictures, which nobody believed, but we all encouraged him to have a look, while David ran to his office for his camera. Paul and I stood there for what seemed a long time watching Anspach stand before each painting with his mouth pursed and his eyebrows slightly lifted, thinking God knows what. In spite of my valid personal reasons for despising him, I understood that I still admired Anspach as a painter, and I wanted to know, once and for all, what he saw when he looked at my work. Paul eased his way to the drinks table and tossed back a full glass of the red wine. David appeared with his camera, and after a brief conversation with Anspach, he called Paul and me over to flank Anspach in front of my painting titled *Welfare*. *Welfare* had an office building in the foreground, from the windows of which floated heavenward a dozen figures of bureaucrats in coats and ties, all wearing shiny black shoes that pointed downward as they went up, resembling the wings of black crows. In David's photograph, two of these figures appear to be rising out of Anspach's head, another issues from one of Paul's ears. Anspach is smiling broadly, showing all his teeth. Paul looks diffident and I look wide-eyed, surprised. When she saw this photo, Yvonne said, "You look like a sheep standing next to a wolf."

After the photograph session, Anspach stepped away from Paul and me and walked off with David, complaining that he had another important engagement. He did not so much as glance back at the door. He had appeared unexpectedly, now he disappeared in the same way. David came back to us with the bemused, wondering expression of one who has met up with a natural force and miraculously survived. He took from his coat pocket a sheet of red adhesive dots and went around the room carefully affixing them to the frames of various pictures. Anspach had bought four of mine and three of Paul's.

I don't attribute my modest success to Anspach, but I guess there are people who do. I attribute it to the paintings, to the quality of the work. I have to do that or I'd just give up. Still there's always that nagging anxiety for any artist who actually begins to sell, that he's compromised something, that he's imitating the fashion. I'm not making a fortune, but I like selling a painting; I like the enthusiasm of the new owner, and I particularly like handing the check to Yvonne. It makes me lazy, though, and complacent. Some days I don't paint at all. I go downtown to check out the competition at the various galleries, drink a few espressos, talk with Paul, who isn't doing as well as I am, but seems incapable of envy, of wishing me anything but well.

I sometimes wonder what van Gogh's paintings would have been like if he had been unable to turn them out fast enough to satisfy an eager, approving public. Suppose he'd been treated as Picasso was, as such a consummate master that any little scribble on a notepad was worth enough to buy the hospital where he died. Would that ear still have had to go?

Yesterday, as I walked out of a café in Chelsea, I ran straight into Anspach, who was coming in. I greeted him politely enough, I always do, but I haven't exchanged more than a few words with him since Maria's death. He pretends not to notice this, or perhaps he thinks it's the inevitable fate of the great artist to be tirelessly snubbed by his inferiors. He asked me to go back in with him, to have an espresso. "You know, I just sold a painting of yours I've had for five years," he said. "Your stock is going up."

It was chilly out, threatening rain, and I'd had an argument with Yvonne that morning. She'd told me I was lazy; that all I did was sleep and drink coffee, which isn't true, but I had defended myself poorly by accusing her of being obsessed with work, money, getting ahead, and we'd parted heatedly, she to work, I to the café. I was not in the mood to have an espresso with Meyer Anspach. He looked prosperous, expansive, pleased with himself. His breath was warm on my face and it smelled bitter, as if he'd been chewing some bitter root.

"It must be nice to have an eye for investments," I said. "It keeps you from having to buy anything you actually care about."

He laughed. "The only paintings I ever want to keep are my own," he said. "I'm always trying to find a way around having to sell them."

"I get it," I said, trying to push past him. "Happy to be of service."

"Looks like I'm the one in service," he observed. "When I sell a painting of yours, it makes everything you do worth more."

This was an intolerable assertion. "Don't do me any favors, OK, Anspach?" I snapped. I had made it to the sidewalk. "I know perfectly well why you bought my paintings."

Anspach came out on the sidewalk with me. He looked eager for a fight. "And why is that?" he said. "What is your theory about that?"

"You want me to forgive you for Maria," I said. "But I never will."

"*You* forgive *me*," he said. "I think it's the other way around."

"What are you talking about?" I said.

"You led her on, Jack, don't tell me you didn't. I was wearing her out and there you were, always ready with the coffee and the bunnies, and trying to feel her up on the subway."

"That's not true," I protested.

"She told me," he said. "She said you were in love with her, and I said, OK, then go, but by the time she got around to making the decision, you were shut up with Yvonne. You closed her out and she gave up. That's why she went off the roof."

"If you'd treated her decently, she wouldn't have needed to turn to me," I said.

"But she did," he shot back. "You made her think she could, and she did. But you couldn't wait for her. You had to have Yvonne. Well, that's fine, Jack. Maria wouldn't have made you happy. She was always depressed, she was always tired. She was never going to do better than waitressing, and sooner or later she was going to go off the roof. Yvonne is a hard worker, and she makes good money. You made the right choice."

"What a swine you are," I said.

He laughed. "You hate me to ease your own conscience," he said. "I was never fooled by you."

"Shut up," I said. I started walking away as fast as I could. I looked back over my shoulder and saw him standing there, smiling at me, as if we were the best of friends. "Shut up," I shouted, and two young women walking toward me paused in their conversation to look me over warily.

I went straight back home, but it took nearly two hours. The subway was backed up; a train had caught fire between 14th

Street and Astor Place. I kept thinking of what Anspach had said, and it made my blood pressure soar. What a self-serving bastard, I thought. As crude as a caveman. I particularly hated his remark about feeling Maria up on the subway. I never did. I never would have. He would have done it, certainly, if he had been with her on those long, cold trips across the river, when she rested her head innocently against his arm, he would have taken advantage of the opportunity, so he assumed I had.

I tortured my memory for any recollection of having brushed carelessly against Maria's breasts. It made me anxious to reach in this way, after so many years, for Maria, and to discover that she was not alive in my memory. I couldn't see her face, remember her perfume. I kept having a vision of a skeleton, which was surely all Maria was now, of sitting on the subway next to a skeleton, and of rubbing my arm against the hard, flat blade of her breastbone.

I spent the rest of the morning trying to paint, but I got nowhere. I could see the painting of Maria's hands clutching the edge of a chute, and behind her, that ominous blue, Anspach's blue period, waiting to swallow her up forever. In the afternoon I picked up my daughter, Bridget, from her school and we spent an hour at the corner library. When we got back home, Yvonne was there, standing at the kitchen counter, chopping something. Was she still mad at me from the morning? I went up beside her on the pretense of washing my hands. "Day OK?" I said.

"Not bad," she said, pleasantly enough. "How about you?"

I sat down at the table and started turning an apple from the fruit bowl round and round in my hands. "I ran into Meyer Anspach today," I said. "He said he sold one of my paintings."

"That's good," she said. She wasn't listening.

"He said Maria was in love with me. He said she thought I

LIMERICK COUNTY LIBRARY 00502229

would wait for her to leave him, but I didn't, and that's why she killed herself."

Yvonne ran some water over her hands, then turned to me, drying them off with a towel. "Maria *was* in love with you," she said. "Are you saying you didn't know that?"

"Of course I didn't know that," I exclaimed. "I still don't know that."

Yvonne gave me a sad smile, such as she sometimes gives Bridget when she gets frustrated by math problems. Then she turned back to the sink. "How could you not have known that?" was all she said.

THE BOWER

Sandra had resisted the idea of the bower. The silk roses entwined in the lattice were moth-eaten and faded, the wood was splattered with mossy green stains, and the ugly bright-pink plastic bow at the top dangled woefully. But now, minus the bow, repainted a pale gray, and bathed in a blue filtered light, it looked pretty good. Jack had created a stone wall, a sheet of plywood cut at a sharp angle which, in a fine bit of *trompe l'oeil*, appeared to recede into the background. "It will keep him from looking like he's wandering in from nowhere," Jack had explained. "And it will frame him and separate him from the rest of the world."

Carter appeared next to the wall, meditatively turning the pages of a book. They had disagreed about the book as well. Should the lovers, if they could be called that, both be wandering around the castle reading books? Sandra thought it was too much, but Jack said it made sense; the prince was a student, after all. Jack wanted something substantial, not a dictionary, but not some flimsy prayerbook, or, as Carter had suggested, a copy of the play. Jack came up with a leatherbound volume of Aristotle, just the right size. "It's my uncle's," he said, unwrapping the book from a neat brown paper package. "He says we can only use it during performances, and I have to wrap it up after each one. It's not that valuable; he's just picky about his books." This made Carter anxious. Wouldn't it put him off balance to rehearse with one book and have a completely different book on the first night? He asked this question, as he asked most questions, with a mild, self-mocking amiability that suggested he would do whatever he was told.

"He's reading a book he's never read before," Jack suggested. "A book that excites him."

Carter rubbed his palm across the coarse blond stubble on his cheek, an inward smile playing on his lips. "And that's why he asks the question," he agreed. "Because of something he just read in the book for the first time." The young men smiled conspiratorially. And that was how Carter arrived at the stress on *is* in *that is the question,* which he delivered with the book raised slightly, lowering his eyes to the page as if to acknowledge it as the inspiration for his soliloquy.

The question was ahead of him now as he passed along the wall. His confidence in his interpretation of the succeeding line was all he had to pull him through the perilous and definitive moment he entered as he turned into the bower; the moment when he must somehow make new the six most famous monosyllables in the English language. He paused, looking up from the page into the middle air, and then he did something Sandra hadn't seen before. He brought his hand to his face and pressed his thumb and forefinger across the bridge of his nose, taking in a slow breath, his eyes closed. He was a man whose thoughts were causing him an unendurable headache. The house was hushed, fascinated. Sandra felt the tiny hairs at the back of her neck rustle. Had he saved up this gesture for this moment, or was he so invested in the character that it had come to him spontaneously?

He is so gifted, Sandra thought, so incredibly gifted. Every now and then a student came along who impressed her, who was "a natural," but she had never seen anything like Carter Sorensen before. The other young men in the program despaired when they knew they would have to share a spotlight with him, though he was so mysteriously egoless and generous he brought out the best in them and they ended up surprising themselves. He had a revved-up clairvoyance during rehearsal, his pale eyes darted a blue flame into the proceedings; the atmosphere simmered, a pot on the boil. Just last week Rowina Murphy, a faculty warhorse who pulled inferior young actors through their lines as if she were harnessed to them, was completely flummoxed when Carter, sensing some visceral resistance as he yanked her about on the bed, said softly, "Mother, give in to me." Tears filled her eyes, her fleshy hand left the pillow and rested on the back of his neck; then, at her touch, Carter recoiled, betrayed, revolted, leaving her trembling with genuine shame. Sandra was so startled she sighed "Yes," and Jack, who was standing next to her, whispered, "Look at Rowina. He's killing her."

The young prince in the bower dropped his fingers from his temple, glanced down at the open book, and then, raising his troubled eyes to the middle distance, every line of his body proclaiming a state of excruciating indecision and torment, his voice pitched just above a whisper, though it could be heard as well on the back row as on the front, he enunciated the simple terms of his predicament. No one in the audience doubted that this was the first time he had ever so irresistibly put the proposition to himself.

At the final curtain, when Carter stepped out to join his dead family and friends, the audience rose to its collective feet, pounding their palms together and shouting their approbation. He took his bows with modest grace, holding out his hands to Ophelia and his mother, as if to acknowledge a debt to his betters. Sandra joined in the applause as she slipped into the aisle and made her way to the front. Carter spotted her, pointed to her, then she was up the steps and on the apron, moving toward him, past the line of actors who applauded her and moved aside to let her pass. Carter gripped her hand as she turned toward the audience; for a moment they were side by side in the spotlight, bowing into a tide of praise that was just beginning to ebb. Sandra was lightheaded, but when she allowed herself a quick peek at Carter, she saw that he was perfectly calm. Always sensitive to the subtlest of motions, he felt her eyes upon him and returned her look with a penetrating bolt of his own. His hand in hers was warm and dry. He had been at the center of a dramatic whirlwind for two and a half hours, and he had not broken a sweat. How old *is* he? Sandra thought unexpectedly.

At the cast party, Carter was fawned upon by a range of young women, from the neurotic Gwen Katz, who had played his Ophelia, to Melanie Davis, a lively, practical redhead who had trained the spotlight steadily upon him. He sipped beer from a can as he thumbed through a stack of tapes looking for something old-fashioned and upbeat, because, he said, he wanted to dance. Everybody knew Carter loved to dance, that he was good at it and could make even a clumsy partner look graceful. As Sandra stood by the drinks table sipping from a plastic cup of cheap red wine, she could feel the anticipation among the young women, like hens ruffling their feathers as the cock steps into the yard. Which one would he choose? As the Surpremes burst upon the room, urging the unfaithful lover to stop in the name of love, Carter, to his credit, Sandra thought, turned to Melanie, and after a brief exchange involving only an invitational raised eyebrow and a nod, led her to the floor.

There was plenty of room to dance. The apartment, which two of the cast members shared, was sparsely furnished. Two couches and a few wooden chairs had been shoved against the wall, an old metal kitchen table with a flowered sheet folded in half as a tablecloth served for the jugs of wine, the plastic cups and paper plates of chips, the tubs of cheese dip and salsa. Other couples strayed onto the floor. Brendan Callahan, the lanky, moody young man who had played Laertes, was, surprisingly, not a bad dancer, though he didn't come close to Carter who was working Melanie through a series of turns with the invisible yet absolute control of a dressage master. Sandra tried to concentrate on a conversation with Rowina, who did not think a budding playwright in the graduate writing program should be allowed to produce his play under the auspices of the Drama department, but her eyes kept drifting back to Carter on the dance floor. Melanie was replaced by Mitzi, the sound director, and then Gwen finally got her chance, but even Carter couldn't make Gwen look more than fitfully animated. Her love affair with her own death was stamped in the slope of her shoulders, the perpetually sidelong cast of her eyes. She had made a doomed victim of Ophelia, a mooning calf bound for slaughter, and Carter had played off of what she gave him. The audience understood that his passion for her was one part sympathy, one part rage. His madness was strategic, purposeful, dangerous, hers was born of self-pity, it was pointless, one more damned perversion of the natural order in the state of Denmark.

Rowina revealed that she had spoken to the department chair about the budding playwright, demanding that she secure the Drama department from the encroaching threat of the English department, but the chair had not shared her anxiety. The playwright had applied for permission to take a graduate directing class, which the chair intended to grant. "This kid has no experience in the theater," Rowina complained. "I read his transcript."

Then Carter, having deposited Gwen upon the couch, where she sank listlessly in the overstuffed cushions, swiftly crossed the room, nodded at Rowina, whose pique at the upstart playwright dissolved, proffered his hand to Sandra, and said, "Would you dance with me?"

She could easily have declined, but that thought only came to her much later. "I'd like that," she replied.

What was the music? It wasn't too fast, not particularly danceable. "My World Is Empty Without You," or "I Hear a Symphony," something bland and preposterous. Sandra was a competent dancer, but as most men were not, she had a tendency to lead, which Carter quickly detected and checked. He brought her hands behind his shoulders and showed her how to shift them to the front, turning away from him at the same time, then twirling out and back into his arms. With a light pressure at her waist, he brought her to his side, then back out again. He raised his arm for the time-honored spin, which she didn't need to be taught. "Good," he said. "You're really a good dancer." He sounded relieved to have found her.

For the rest of the evening, apart from breaks at the drinks table, Sandra danced with Carter. The music was always upbeat; they were never swaying in one another's arms; when they were on the floor they were always in motion, becoming more synchronized, smoother with each number. It looked like good clean fun. The partygoers smiled upon this couple, the director and her protégé, the former safely married with children, a marriage universally envied for its domestic tranquility, and the latter a well-mannered, handsome, agreeable young man who had no particular girlfriend and was therefore, in some quarters, believed to be homosexual. But each time Sandra's hand slid down Carter's lean, muscular shoulder, whenever his fingers closed tightly around her waist and drew her close to his side, she knew there was nothing innocent about this dancing. As she filled her plastic cup with cheap wine, odd questions darted across her consciousness. Why wasn't Carter interested in the spirited conversation of his peers, who were gathered in little clutches about the room laughing and flirting, going over every detail of the play, of their part in Carter's success? Could there be any truth to the rumors that he was gay? How old was he, anyway? Surely he was at least twenty-five.

When she was dancing with him, these questions disappeared, and she was lost in the pleasure of moving about confidently, her partner directing her with subtle cues. Their eyes seldom crossed, they hardly spoke. There were other couples on the floor, some perfectly adequate, but whenever Sandra took a break to drink more, she observed that there wasn't much in the way of electricity between these couples, indeed they seemed to have found a way to dance in tandem, without actually acknowledging one another. Why? They were young, blood was coursing through their veins. On stage they were exuberant, kinetic, full of life, but here, celebrating a successful communal endeavor, they seemed muffled, as if they had recently met one another.

Still they were dedicated to their party and it went on late into the evening. Rowina Murphy gave out at last and waved to Sandra as she pulled on her coat at the door. "Have fun," she said. Gwen, looking out the door as Rowina passed, reported that it was raining, news that had a sobering effect upon Sandra. She had walked the four blocks to the party, her car was in the parking lot at the college, her house six blocks in the opposite direction. She didn't have an umbrella or a jacket. She could have rushed out after Rowina and asked her for a ride to her car, but she didn't. Did she have some romantic image of herself as Gene Kelly, splashing through the puddles singing, "Come on with the rain, I've a smile on my face"? Carter was going through the tapes again, looking for an Al Green compendium; Gwen and Brendan stood by chatting with him. When he crossed the room to lead Sandra back to the floor, they began rummaging through the coats on the rack near the door. "Let's stay together," Al Green intoned, which made Sandra laugh because she knew about the girlfriend who had poured a pot of steaming grits over the singer while he sat in the bathtub, an experience which had led him to a religious conversion. She told this story to Carter as he passed her from hand to hand, and he laughed. "Grits!" he said. "If only Hamlet had thought of that."

By the time the song was over, another departing group was at the door, which, when opened, elicited cries of dismay; it was a downpour. "What time is it?" Sandra asked Carter, who smiled at her blissfully and said, "I have no idea."

"I can't get home without getting soaked," she said, as the partygoers rushed out into the rain. "I didn't bring my car."

"I have mine," Carter said, snapping her out and back again. "I'll drive you as soon as we finish this dance."

"Great," Sandra said. "I'd appreciate it."

The car was an old Honda Civic, redolent of mildew and orange air freshener, the original upholstery covered in cheap black and orange polka-dot nylon covers. Carter made no apologies for it. "Your house is on Livingston, isn't it?" he said as he started the engine and yanked the seat belt across his chest. Sandra followed his example, but she couldn't get the buckle into the lock. Her brain was buzzing now with various lines of inquiry, the seat belt latch being of a minor order. How did Carter know what street she lived on? Shouldn't she tell him to drive her to her car instead of her house? If he drove her to her house, he would see that it was completely dark, because Barry had taken the boys to his mother's in New Jersey for the weekend. Of course, she could say the family was asleep, as indeed they would have been had they been home, but wouldn't he wonder why no one had left a light on for her? And by what arcane reasoning did she owe Carter Sorensen an explanation for the fact that her house was dark? A final, clearly important question had to do with how much wine she had actually drunk and whether she might not weave or even stumble up the sidewalk to her front door. This was also the reason she should not attempt to drive her car.

Like a thunderbolt, Carter's hand came down upon hers, easing the buckle out of her grip and securing it with a metallic snap into the lock. Momentarily her head cleared. "It's the last house on the right," she said. Carter flipped the windshield wipers on and, with the reassuring rhythmic slap-slap of the rubber blades against the glass, they took off into the night.

Carter drove a block without speaking. Sandra noticed that there was no radio in the car, that something heavy, it sounded like a pipe, was rolling around loose in the back, that the floor was disturbingly close to the road. "That was fun," she said to say something. "I haven't danced like that in a long time."

"Your husband doesn't dance?" Carter said.

"Barry? No, he's not a dancer."

"That's too bad," Carter said. They had reached her street and he turned onto it, shifting the gears easily. "People should dance."

Sandra chuckled. "That sounds like a prescription," she said.

"It is," he said. "It's a good prescription."

"You're the doctor of dance," she said.

"This is it, right?" Carter said, turning into the drive. Her house leaped into the headlights, blurred by the rain, solid, dark, the windows glinting sinisterly, the climbing rose on the trellis near the kitchen door as dense and menacing as the briar thicket around Sleeping Beauty's castle. "Looks like everyone's asleep," Carter observed.

"They're not here," Sandra said. "They've all gone to my mother-in-law's for the weekend. I'm going down to join them tomorrow."

"Where does she live?"

"New Jersey," Sandra said. "On the shore. It's the last weekend they can still swim."

"You have two boys, right?"

"Yes," she replied. How did he know this, she thought, and then, but everybody knows it. "Marco and Duncan, they're seven and eleven," she said.

"Good swimmers?" Carter asked.

Sandra fumbled on the floor for her purse. It was a short dash to the porch, and she understood that it was time to make it. "Yes, very good," she said. "Duncan more than Marco. Duncan is a fish."

"I don't swim," Carter informed her.

"Nor I," she said, pulling the purse into her lap. He was beginning to strike her as a little odd; she was, at that moment, very willing to leave him to his own promising young life. "Well, I'd better go in," she said. "Thanks so much for driving me."

"My pleasure," Carter said.

Then she couldn't find the door handle, and Carter had to reach across her to open it. "Oh, thanks," she said. She pushed the door open, put one foot out into the rain, pushed off the car

floor with the other, slammed her shoulder into the upper edge of
the door frame, and collapsed on her side in the wet gravel.

Before she was even sure what had happened. Carter was out
of the car, rushing to her aid. She sat up, brushed the gravel from
her hands and her shoulder. He bent over her, trying to pull her
up by her elbows. "Sandra," he said. "Are you OK?"

She got to her knees. "I'm fine," she said. "I'm not used to such
a low car, I guess." She stood up. Her shoulder hurt; there would
be an ugly bruise. Carter passed his arm around her back just
as he had when they were dancing, but it felt different, more
intimate, almost an embrace. "Let's get you inside," he said.

As they made their way up the drive, the rain wilted their
clothes, their hair. Behind the rose trellis in the safety of the
porch, Sandra dug in her purse for the key, while Carter shook
himself like a dog. She turned the key in the lock and pushed
open the door into the dark kitchen. Carter followed her inside.
"You should sit down," he said. "Let me get you some ice."

She switched on the light by the table, which was dim—one of
the big problems with the kitchen, not enough light—and sank
onto a chair. Her right shin hurt and an exploration with her
fingers revealed that her stocking was shredded and sticky wet. "I
think I cut my leg," she said. Carter had gone to the sink, taken up
a dish towel, and dumped a few ice cubes into it from the server
on the refrigerator door. "I'm bringing you some ice," he said.
She looked up to see him carefully wrapping the ice, the rain
streaming from his hair onto the counter.

"What we need is towels," she said. "The bathroom is right
there, on the right."

He went out and reappeared with a towel, which he patted
against his skull. A feminine method, Sandra thought, the one she
used herself. He came to her then, the towel in one hand, the

cloth-wrapped ice in the other. She took the towel and applied it to her hair while he kneeled on the floor before her, inspecting the shin. "This is a nasty cut," he said.

Sandra looked down at him, feeling grateful; he was so motherly, the opposite of the young man he had been a few hours before, standing in the bower, bringing his fingertips to the bridge of his nose in an agony of indecision. "It's not important," she said. "I'll take care of it."

Carter looked up at her with an expression that she found unreadable. She brought her hand to his shoulder, bending down closer to him. "It's all right," she said, and they kissed.

They kissed. Or was it that he kissed her and she responded, or wasn't it rather that she kissed him and, after a nanosecond of undisguised astonishment, he responded? These questions did not occur to Sandra at the moment, but much later, much too late, they came up forcefully. She was never to know the answer. In the next moment the kiss turned into an embrace and they tumbled to the floor, where they tore at each other's clothes until all the significant bits were exposed and, with groans of passion as well as pain, for the floor was hard and the chair legs seemed to be everywhere, they satisfied the curiosity they had spent the evening exacerbating on the dance floor. When they were done, Sandra was on her back, Carter collapsed across her, his face hidden against her shoulder. She brought her hand tentatively to the nape of his neck, waiting to come to her senses. Would Barry know at once, she wondered, just by looking at her? Carter lifted his head, smiled at her, then hid his face again, his lips pressed to her ear. "I can't believe we just did that," he said.

"I'm sorry," Sandra said. Then, recognizing this as an insensitive and unloverlike remark, she added, "I couldn't resist."

"Me neither," he said.

*

On the following Monday, Sandra stopped off at the departmental office, helped herself to a cup of departmental coffee, and drifted to the file cabinet where the student records were stored. Casually she slid open the heavy drawer, casually she pulled a few files and slipped them into her canvas briefcase. Glenda, the secretary, hardly looked up as she passed out into the hall, so there was no need for her to say in a voice of long suffering, "Recommendation time," but she did. Nor, after she had scuttled along the hall, clutching the briefcase tightly as if it contained an explosive device, was it necessary for her to close her office door. She sat at her desk, extracted the folders, pushed aside the ones that didn't interest her, opened the one that did, and, resting her chin in her hands, her elbows propped on the desktop, scanned the page before her hurriedly. Then she covered her eyes with her fingertips and moaned.

He was twenty-one, ten years older than Duncan, fifteen years younger than she was. He had come to the college straight out of his prep school, one of the less tony, more socially-conscious schools, stashed away in a picturesque New England backwater, a spacious, landscaped campus with bubbling streams, towering sugar maples, and vast stone Thornfield-hall-style buildings: Sandra had toured it once, thinking it might be right for Duncan. Carter's family address was New Jersey, so he'd been a boarder. His mailing address was on a street near her own, an apartment, 2B, doubtless in one of the large old homes that had been cut up haphazardly by owners who charged exorbitant rents and didn't bother keeping up the place because students didn't care and seldom complained. Carter probably had a roommate, maybe two.

Sandra opened her eyes and re-examined the numbers in the

date-of-birth box, as if they might have changed since last she looked, but they stubbornly insisted that Carter was twenty-one, just barely; his birthday was in September. "At least he's legal," she said ruefully. A hot flush enveloped her face, blurring her vision. What had she done? And what should she do now?

Carter hadn't stayed long after they got up off the floor. Sandra offered him a glass of wine, coffee, food, all of which he politely declined. They sat at the table, pulling their clothes back on, uncomfortable now with each other, though Sandra noticed that the atmosphere was distinctly friendly. "I'd better go," he said as she patted down her hair, pulled at her sleeves. "I guess so," she replied, looking up into his amused, kindly regard. They laughed. She followed him to the door, where he turned and kissed her again. "Thank you," he said, and she replied, laughing again, "Anytime." Then he was gone. She turned out the lights and crept upstairs, keeping her brain from any reproachful introspection by concentrating on washing her face, brushing her teeth, hanging up her clothes, putting on her nightgown. She stretched out under the sheets—how good it felt to be in her big bed alone—and fell into a deep dreamless sleep from which she woke with a throbbing head, possessed of an almighty thirst.

Barry did not know as soon as he saw his wife, nor did the boys appear to feel any alteration in the aura of affection and approval that emanated from their mother. All three greeted her arrival at the shore as that which was to be expected. Moira, Barry's mother, was not more curious about Sandra's doings than she had ever been. Her garden continued to be first in all her considerations, her son and grandsons of secondary interest, her daughter-in-law came in somewhere behind the dog. As Sandra strolled along the beach with her husband, inspecting the shells and bits of sea drift that it was Marco's pleasure to display to her, she could almost believe she was unchanged, that what she now thought of as "the incident of the floor" had never happened, or, if it could be proved to have occurred, that it had no weight, was not, already, a burden. Dinner was relaxed, Barry grilled everything on Moira's deck, there was good wine, and then a family stroll to the ice-cream parlor for dessert. As usual, she and Barry stayed up after everyone was in bed, drinking brandy on the deck, talking over the day, the boys' antics, plans for the future. It was hot, the moon was full and high, the waves rolled in and out, industriously cleaning the shoreline. "How did the play go?" Barry inquired off-handedly, and Sandra replied without hesitation, "Really well. Better than hoped. Everyone died beautifully."

"Good," Barry said. "Good house?"

"Excellent," she said. "Very attentive. Packed too."

"That's great," he said and changed the subject, thus delivering his wife from the threat of having to speak the name she didn't feel confident to pronounce.

In bed Barry turned to her, nuzzling his face against her back, bringing her in close by grasping her waist in both hands and pulling. She welcomed his embrace, relieved to find it so familiar, easy and warm. What followed was equally reassuring, the snug fit of their practiced lovemaking, the amusing necessity to keep her voice down because Moira's room was across the hall. Afterward Barry rolled onto his back, breathing hard. "Funny," he said when he had stopped gasping for breath, "how fucking in my mother's house is still so exciting."

Sandra chuckled. "It's because it was forbidden for so long," she said. And then, as her husband drifted off to sleep, she listened to what she had just said and felt a chill in the vicinity of her heart.

Was that it? she thought as she turned a page of Carter's file and noticed that he had not declared himself a theater major until the end of his sophomore year. Was she feeling so flush with energy and excitement, was she in such a remarkably good, albeit agitated mood, because she had done something transgressive and gotten away with it? And if it never happened again, shouldn't that be enough? Or would she, having stumbled into previously undreamed-of territory, be so overmastered by curiosity and the thrill of discovery that she would be drawn, again and again, a little farther across the border?

There was a sharp rap on her office door, followed by three timid taps, the knuckles of two fingers making hesitant contact with the wood. Sandra closed the folder abruptly and slid it into the desk drawer as she called out, in what she hoped was a normal, guiltless voice, "Come in." The doorknob turned, the door slid open to reveal Carter standing in the frame. He was wearing a black turtleneck sweater which made his fair skin, light hair, and eyes look ethereal, angelic. What woman wouldn't envy those cheekbones, Sandra thought inappropriately, for his expression was serious; his movements, as he stepped inside and closed the door carefully behind him, evinced a controlled urgency. He leaned against the door, pushing back a bundle of his abundant, disorderly hair with the back of his hand, giving her a wan smile. He hasn't been sleeping well, Sandra thought.

"We have to talk," he said.

The lovers met frequently, two or three times a week, trysts that required careful planning. In the morning, once Barry and the boys were off, it was possible to meet at Sandra's house, but it was tricky, as her neighbors on both sides worked at the college. Carter came in through the backyard, shielded from view by a hedge, let himself in at the mud-room door, and, keeping low, passed down the hall to the TV room, where Sandra had drawn the curtains and sat on the couch in the gloom waiting for him. His attic apartment was the place for meetings in the evening, but it was dangerous because Brendan Callahan lived just below. Sandra pulled Brendan's schedule and they chose a time when he had a film class, from seven to nine, Tuesdays and Thursdays, but this didn't keep Sandra from rushing past Brendan's door as if a tiger might suddenly pounce upon her. As time passed, Sandra was to discover that she and Carter had largely divergent views, but on one thing they were in complete accord, the necessity for absolute secrecy. No one must know, and no one did know, with the exception of Carter's older brother in New Jersey, in whom he had confided. "What did he say?" Sandra asked, when Carter told her of this conversation. She was curled up next to him on the mattress that served as his bed. "He said, 'A teacher, that's not good.'"

"And what did you say?" she asked.

Carter was on his back, gazing up at the ceiling. He opened his eyes wide, without looking at her. "I said, 'I know it.'"

It wasn't good, they both knew it, but for the first few weeks it was fun. Sandra discovered that she was a good liar, and also that her husband was incurious about her. Eventually she understood that Barry didn't ask exacting questions because he trusted her, but while she was constructing unnecessary, never-to-be-tested alibis, she was miffed by his failure to notice that his busy wife was busier than a wife should be.

He did notice, everyone noticed, that she was looking exceptionally well, that her skin glowed, her hair, which she wore down more than she had before, gleamed, that her figure was lithe and strong. She attributed this to the tennis she was playing while Duncan had his class at the college, and to the running she had taken up in the evenings, when Brendan Callahan was nodding through his film class.

39

Though the lovers didn't speak of it, they knew their affair had a clock and that it would run out, at the latest, in May, when Carter graduated. A few weeks after the incident on the floor, Sandra arrived at Carter's apartment with a bottle of champagne tucked inside her jacket to celebrate his acceptance into a prestigious acting program in New York. She didn't point out that the city was less than two hours away, that she went in two or three times a month on various errands, that part of her pleasure in his success was the proximity it promised. She pushed certain facts—that the city was so expensive Carter would require a roommate, and that Barry often accompanied her on her excursions—out of her mind. Carter was delighted with the champagne; it was expensive, not something any of the young women who admired him could afford. He played a Johnny Hartman CD, "Of all things," Sandra said, and they danced, very close this time, and drank the wine. Carter was talkative, full of plans. He would be meeting some of the great actors of the stage, trying out for parts in professional theaters; by the time he graduated, in only two years, he would be in Actor's Equity. Eventually they fell upon the mattress, though Sandra had a sense of having to lead him to it. He had talked so long there was very little time left, and no sooner were they done than she had to leave. She pulled on her running clothes and tied up her laces, still breathless, while Carter lay propped on the pillows, examining a bruise on his bicep. "I think Brendan suspects us," he said.

Sandra finished her bow, taking in this information cautiously because it struck her as potentially explosive. "Has he seen me coming in?"

"I don't know," Carter said. "I don't think so." She was sitting on the edge of the mattress, her back to him, and as he spoke, her

eyes wandered over the furnishings of his room. "He just brings
you up a lot; I think he has a crush on you. Yesterday he started
going on about how we were dancing at the party. 'You danced
with her all night,' he said, and then he asked me why I never go
out with anyone."

"What did you say?"

"I said I like to keep to myself and he said, 'Right.' Something
about the way he was talking made me think he knows."

Sandra's eyes had come to rest on Carter's ticket collection,
which covered the surface of a green plastic table under the
window. He collected theatre tickets and arranged them in the
order of his preference, which was constantly changing, sometimes radically, each time he saw a new play. A play in the bottom
ranks might suddenly advance to the front. This had amused her
at first, it struck her as boyish, but now she thought only that it
was odd. Bizarre was the word that came to mind. "What should
we do?" she said.

"I think I'd better start going out more."

She turned to look at Carter. His expression was unconcerned,
sleepy. Just past his ear was the clock.

"Good God," Sandra said. "I've got to run."

Carter was not in any of Sandra's classes, but the college was
small, the theater students cliquish, so hardly a day passed when
she did not see him in some public setting: at try-outs, or in the
audience of studio productions, or holding court among his
favorites in the student lounge or the snack bar. Sandra was
teaching basic acting and directing *Waiting for Godot*. Carter was
not in *Godot*, but Brendan Callahan was, which made Sandra
uncomfortable, tongue-tied and diffident. The spirits of her
students soared and dived around her; being in their midst had

once been the source of her energy, but now she felt impatient with them, as if they were draining her with their antics, their shouting, their outbursts of laughter, tears, or song, their passion for all things theatrical, their exuberant camaraderie. They didn't notice anything amiss; they wanted to please her. She was their director, and her reputation was solid. Everyone knew how close she had come to the success they dreamed of, how well-connected she was still in the complex arena they longed to enter. No one asked why she had left it. Her husband, the elegant, popular dean of liberal arts, her good-looking, athletic boys, her comfortable house and tenured position, these were clearly reason enough.

And so she had thought herself, but as the weeks slipped by and Carter appeared in public always with the same young woman—a girl really—a freshman with the fair skin, thick black hair, and light eyes of the Iberian peninsula, Sandra began, for the first time, to consider why she had drifted into the safe harbor of teaching, marriage, children, instead of steering for the tempestuous seas which Carter proposed now to navigate. He would be successful, she did not doubt it, perhaps more successful than he could yet imagine. He had already shown a survivor's instinct by choosing only totally inappropriate women who could easily be left behind. The beautiful freshman would recover in a matter of weeks, and as for Sandra, his secret adventure, it could not be imagined that she would do aught but bid him a sad, fond farewell.

But what if she didn't? She was jogging down the alley behind her house, turning into the avenue which led to Carter's street, when this thought came to her. It was raining, as it had been on that first night. Soaked to her skin she would rush up the stairs and into his arms. "This is commendable devotion to the fitness routine," Barry had observed as she sat at the kitchen table tying up her shoes. She had not been alone with Carter for ten days. "I like running in the rain," she said. As luck would have it, this was true.

What if she didn't bid Carter a tearful farewell? she asked herself again. Her shoes slapped a crisp refrain against the wet pavement. *Why not? Why not?*

Why not go with him to New York? She could protect him, assist him, support him until his talent was recognized, acclaimed, and then she would be his companion, the one who had seen him through. She wouldn't be far from the boys; she could commute to her job. The boys could spend weekends with her in the city, they'd love that. Barry would be heartbroken, angry, he might never forgive her, but there were half a dozen single women on the faculty who would be eager to comfort him; he'd have to fight them off, and in spite of himself, he'd enjoy that. It would be difficult at first; they'd have to keep their plans a secret until after Carter moved, but surely it was possible, and what a fabulous adventure it would be, what a liberating change. As she turned the last corner and saw the light in Carter's window just ahead, she had a vision of being on a stage with him, an attentive audience breathing out there, thrilling to the electricity between them, this marvelous couple, who, everyone knew, had fallen in love when he was in school and she was directing him in a production of *Hamlet*. Foolishness, Sandra told herself, but, as she pulled open the screen and took the stairs two at a time, past Brendan Callahan's door and on to the top landing where Carter's door stood slightly ajar, she examined this fantasy with shy pleasure. She pushed the door open, laughing, breathless, eager for his embrace.

Carter was standing near the window, his back to her, bent

over the plastic table with a slip of cardboard in one hand. He moved the ticket over the arrangement thoughtfully, as if it were a jigsaw piece. "Just one moment," he said, without turning to her.

They never argued. Sandra lay sprawled across Carter's mattress while he explained that his girlfriend was very jealous; he'd really never seen anything like it, and he had agreed that she would move out of her dorm and come live with him. "I'm sorry to make you unhappy," he said, stroking her hair while she sobbed into his pillow.

"It's not your fault," she said. "It's inevitable. I'm just crying because I don't have any choice."

But that wasn't exactly it. She was weeping because, had she been offered a choice, she might have destroyed her happiness forever.

Sandra spent the rest of the semester picking over the affair obsessively, like a monkey grooming her offspring. She admitted that, from the start, she had overpowered Carter, literally as well as figuratively, because she was bigger than he was. Their lovemaking had been athletic; he invariably ended up with some bruise or bite mark that distressed him. She had scoffed at his complaints. She reran snippets of their conversations and found solid evidence that he had tired of the affair quickly, within a matter of days, but he had acquiesced to her enthusiasm and allowed himself to be swept along like some clever crab scuttling along the shore while the waves crash in all around. He was not the obsessive, introspective, intelligent, and passionate young prince who longed to take action, to seize his life, but rather a boy with little experience of the world, self-centered and over-confident. When Sandra spotted him now, in the boisterous company of his friends, the pretty, doubtful girlfriend never far from his side, she was transfixed by a complex of emotions: longing, sadness, jealousy, anxiety, welling up one after the other like demons leaping from a deep reservoir of shame.

He was gone over the Christmas holiday, a solid month in which she shopped, baked and celebrated with grim determination. Then he was back, the pretty freshman still cleaving to him—had she taken him home to meet her parents?—still the focus of departmental expectations, the subject of hopeful murmurs at the beginning and end of faculty meetings. Sandra was teaching only one class, having agreed to a rotation of administrative duties. Carter directed a lively production of *Man and Superman* which Sandra attended, rising to her feet with the rest of the audience when he bounded up the stairs to take his bows. She contrived to miss his final triumph as Mercutio in *Romeo and Juliet*, a role, the college newspaper opined, he invested with "savage grandeur."

At graduation she had every hope of missing him in the crowd, but after the ceremony, as she and Barry were threading their way across the lawn, balancing plastic champagne cups and paper plates loaded with cake for the boys, there he was in his cap and gown, laughing at something an elegant blonde woman had just said to him. "Here you are," he said, waving them in with both hands. "I'm so glad I found you. I want you to meet my parents. Mother, this is Sandra Blakely, my teacher, and this is Barry Blakely, our dean; this is my mother Elizabeth and my dad Evan Sorenson." A small, dapper man, with a double chin and quick black eyes, whom Sandra had failed to notice, overshadowed as he invariably must have been by the brilliance of his wife and son, stepped forward, his hand extended. Then, as they all realized Sandra and Barry had not one hand free between them, there was a general burst of nervous laughter. "A pleasure to meet you,"

Barry said, "Carter is our rising star, but you probably know that. You must be very proud of him."

Sandra stood smiling, nodding her agreement with her husband. She couldn't look at Carter, nor did she want to, for she was mesmerized by his mother. Elizabeth Sorenson was taller than both her husband and her son, willowy yet athletic; Sandra could imagine her on the tennis court, graceful and cool, slamming the ball across the net with hardly a flicker of her perfect eyebrows. The pale eyes, heavy blonde hair, and high cheekbones that were effeminate on her son gave her the air of a startled wild creature, irresistible yet unapproachable, likely to bolt. These eyes settled on Sandra with mild expectancy, so that she racked her brain for something to say and blurted out, in the midst of the father's description of his satisfaction with the college, "Carter is a wonderful actor."

Elizabeth smiled, then bent her curious regard upon her son, as if to discover in him evidence of this charge. "He does seem to love acting," she said.

"I do love it," Carter said, and Sandra was forced to look at him. Their eyes crossed without meeting, like cats, Sandra thought, and then mercifully Marco appeared in a gap among the suits and gowns, calling, "Mom, come see this." Everyone laughed, presumably at a boy's urgent need to report the world to his mother. "Please excuse me," Sandra said, going off to her son, and Barry, repeating his conviction that it had been a pleasure to meet the Sorensons, drifted after her across the bright green lawn. Sandra glanced back at her husband, but her gaze went past him to the proud family. The parents were conversing, their heads inclined toward each other, his up, hers down. Carter stood off to the side looking directly at Sandra. Their eyes met, held; foolishly Sandra lifted her plastic cup in a silent toast. Her heel snagged in the soft turf and she stumbled a step, righting herself as Marco ran toward her, eager to relieve her of the cake. "Mom, come and see," he crowed. "The graduates are jumping in the pond."

Eight years later, at a hiring convention in Chicago, Sandra found herself in a hotel bar, across a marble table from Brendan Callahan, who was applying for an entry-level position at three different colleges. Brendan, whom Sandra had discounted as an actor, had been reasonably successful. After graduating he had landed a small role in an off-Broadway play that had had a long run; then he got a TV role as the insouciant doorman of an apartment building in which three famous comedians tried to steal one another's material. This show was short-lived, but it paid well, allowing Brendan to do some directing, which, he now confessed over his pint of dark beer, was what he really wanted to do. He had married, his wife wanted to get out of the city, and he had decided that teaching might be a good way to go. Sandra had been his inspiration in school. He wanted to be what she had been to her students.

Sandra recalled Carter's remark, "I think he has a crush on you," which made her smile. It was as if she had suddenly heard Carter's voice, and Brendan seemed to hear it too, because, after a pause in which he swallowed a quarter of his beer, he said, "I saw Carter Sorenson last spring. He's doing pretty well."

"Is he?" Sandra replied. "Where is he now?"

"He's in Spokane. He teaches at a private high school there. He's married now, he has a little daughter, his wife is a librarian at the school."

"Spokane?" Sandra said.

"After he left the acting program he went out to California. I think he just drifted around a bit, couldn't get work, then he met

Marion and they moved up to Spokane so he could finish his master's. She has family there."

"He didn't finish the program?" Sandra said.

"He didn't go back after the accident," Brendan said, setting his beer down carefully. "Don't you know about the accident?"

The accident. It was in the spring of Carter's first year in New York City. His older brother was getting married, and it had fallen to Carter to deliver the bride to the wedding in Vermont. He'd rented a car, left the city in the afternoon, heading for New Haven, where the bride—her name was Ann—was a student at Yale. They were old friends; their parents' summer houses stood across a field dotted with cows in the picturesque hills of Vermont.

It was a dreary day, chilly and raining in Connecticut. By the time they got to Massachusetts, the rain had turned to a slushy snow. The interstate was so bad cars were pulled over, lights flashing. The plows weren't out yet; the traffic slowed to a crawl. They pulled off at Northampton and called ahead to say they were safe, but they were hungry and had decided to have something to eat. Perhaps the weather would improve. Ann's mother encouraged them to get hotel rooms and stay there, the wedding was not until the next afternoon, they could easily make it in the morning, but Carter said no, he thought they could do it; he had seen two plows going out as they drove into town; it would just be slow. They ate dinner at a diner; Carter drank a lot of coffee and they headed out again. It was dark by then, the snow had turned to needles of ice, but after a few difficult miles they got behind a plow and made it to the Vermont border. The plow took the last exit and then, to their relief, all precipitation stopped. The blackness overhead took on a sheen, as if the sky itself had frozen. The traffic thinned out. Carter was driving slowly for fear of ice or deer. They were less than a mile from the exit, on an incline that spanned a rocky ravine at the bottom of which churned a swollen creek. The front wheels skidded on an ice patch; the car careened smoothly through the flimsy guard rail and pitched off the road. The back tires caught on the rail; for a few moments they were suspended in space, then the metal gave and the car plunged down upon the granite boulders, coming to rest topside down in the icy water which poured in through the smashed windows. Carter got out, he didn't remember how, and dragged himself up onto the creek bed. That was when he heard Ann screaming.

"He told me he'd never heard anything like her screams," Brendan said. "It was hideous. It wasn't terror, she wasn't calling for help. He said it was 'mortal agony.' He thought he'd died and waked up in hell."

Sandra sipped her drink, trying to ward off the chill that had invaded her bones. "What happened to her?" she said quietly.

"She'd been thrown out of the car somehow and she was trapped under the back wheel. It was dark. Carter couldn't find her at first, then, when he did, he couldn't do anything but keep her head above the water until the police came. It was hours before they got her out. They had to get a crane to lift the car, then they called in a helicopter."

"Did she survive?"

"No," Brendan said.

The hotel had been built at the turn of the twentieth century; the rooms were large, the bathtub immense. As Sandra stood pouring the fragrant salts provided by the management over the rising water, she recalled a story she had heard of an English professor who had drowned in such a tub, during a convention just like this one. He'd had a few drinks at the bar too; then, imprudently, he'd taken a sleeping pill before settling into a hot bath. Clearly a desperate insomniac, Sandra thought when she heard this story, and she was sympathetic because sleep had become more and more elusive in the last few years. "The burning brain," Barry called it, that flames up at three a.m. and incinerates reason. She had not yet resorted to pills. Carefully she stepped over the high wall of the tub and lowered herself into the water. When she turned off the tap the silence of the room flooded in and she sat quite still, watching the last drops plop from the faucet onto the oily surface of the water. It was a luxury to be alone in a hotel room, or any room for that matter. The boys were always banging in and out at home, students never stopped appearing at the office door, and at night there was always Barry settling in beside her, comfortable and warm, like a drowsy puppy; he was asleep almost as soon as his head touched the pillow.

Sandra eased down beneath the water. The tub was long enough to stretch her legs out entirely. She dropped the wash-cloth into the steamy water, wrung it out, and spread it across her breasts, breathing a deep sigh. Brendan's story had shocked her in so many ways she felt her neck and shoulders aching as if she'd taken a series of blows.

A line from a letter she had written surfaced menacingly. "A student about whose future I am entirely confident." It wasn't a letter for Carter; for reasons that were bitterly obvious, he'd never asked her for one; but it could have been. It was a line she would never use again. Carter's fate made a mockery of such sanguine predictions. She imagined the letter written by the designer of that fate: "This student will survive a scene of horror and be left, as survivors are notoriously reputed to be, no matter how persistently the term 'accident' be applied, with the certainty that he was responsible for that horror."

Sandra pulled the cloth from her chest and spread it over her face, fighting back tears in the moist darkness. Poor innocent young man. What must be his suffering still, what poisonous dreams must fill his nights, what images leap up unexpectedly in the course of his days?

Whenever Sandra thought of Carter, which was, she admitted, not often, a particular memory came to the fore; it was the way she could finally see his face. Interestingly it was not from any occasion of intimacy, nor could she find him in those overheated exchanges of looks in public; it was not, and perhaps this explained it, lodged in any recollection that involved his looking back at her. It was that moment when he stepped into the bower, studying his book, pondering his options, to suffer in silence or to act, to live or to die. His fate is already sealed, obvious to everyone but him, yet some awful intimation of doom lifts his eyes from his book, his hand comes to his smooth brow, he presses his fingers to the bridge of his nose and sighs. It's almost as if he knows, but of course he doesn't know. He cannot see what Sandra sees now as she pulls the cloth from her eyes and sits up in the hotel tub, feeling the grip of panic in her chest and deeper, in her entrails, as a new vision of Carter comes to her. It is pitch-dark, bitterly cold, an icy wind numbs his face, his fingers; he is on his hands and knees on frozen ground, clutching at stones; his fingers slip, he falls. There is a sound rending the air, a sound so terrifying every cell of his body directs him to turn away, but he has no choice. He has entered into a scene from which there is no escape, it is his part, it has been waiting for him, it is his alone. Resolutely, hopelessly, he gets back up on his hands and knees and crawls across the stage to meet it.

BEETHOVEN

"There's something Oriental about you," Philip said as I got out of the bed. This was in the 60s, before Oriental became the wrong word for Asian. As there is nothing remotely Asian about my appearance—I'm blonde, blue-eyed—I concluded that Philip was referring to some perception he had about my character.

Philip was desperate, but I didn't know it yet. As I passed the easel and the paint truck on my way to the bathroom, I had to step over a stack of wallpaper books. This was Phil's latest innovation, painting on wallpaper samples. His friend Sid couldn't stop ridiculing him about the wallpaper, but Philip said Sid was just jealous. Though they seemed to dislike each other, Phil and Sid went out drinking regularly and these evenings inevitably degenerated into bitter arguments that left Philip muttering until dawn. "Why do you go with him?" I asked once, to which he responded, with no hint of irony, "We're friends."

Phil was thirty, I was barely twenty. Everything about him interested me. He was a man, not a boy, he was my introduction to the adult world I longed to enter, the real world, apart from college, which I'd left after one year, feeling the need to throw myself, if not upon thorns, at least upon something that would leave an impression. My parents, at first furious, then disappointed, had become resigned. I was required to visit them once a week, Sunday dinner, which was fine with me as I was eating poorly on my own and I enjoyed being idolized by my two younger brothers who thought that having a job and an apartment in the French Quarter was the absolute limit of sophistication. The fact that my job was waiting tables and my apartment a dark, roach-infested hole did not dampen their enthusiasm. After dinner they walked me to the bus stop, regaling me with stories about the trials of high school, which they made me promise never to tell my parents. When the bus came, I hugged them as if I was going off into a perilous adventure instead of just across town to meet Philip at a smoke-filled bar, to watch Philip work his way down one more rung of the ladder that stretched between desperation and despair.

I had begun to understand that my expectations of the world were unrealistic. I had imagined that, as a working single woman, I would attract the attention of a working single man, we would fall in love, and he would ask me to throw my lot in with him. Then I would leave my apartment and move in to his. I wasn't picturing anything palatial; two rooms would have been accept-able, especially if there were windows. Philip's friend Sid lived with his girlfriend Wendy in two rooms. They had a tiny kitchen, a decent bath and their bedroom opened onto a seedy patio. I assumed, for no reason, that the place had been Sid's first; that Wendy had come to him there. Later, of course, I found out the reverse was true. Now it strikes me that the most touching thing about myself in this period was this pathetic assumption, which must have come from reading fairy tales about princesses who, like rabbits, are always taken to their husbands' abodes for breeding purposes.

Philip's apartment constituted a serious obstacle to the main-tenance of my supposition. We lived in the same run-down building. He was in the hot stuffy attic at the top; I was at the bottom, near the narrow side alley where the perpetually over-flowing garbage cans were lined up, lovingly attended by swarms of flies and the occasional rat. That was where I met Phil, struggling to drag his can out to the street. "I'll help you, if you'll help me," I said. He started; he hadn't noticed my approach, and set his can down hard on the concrete, regarding me reproach-fully. I stepped toward him into a thin slice of light that filtered through the wrought-iron gate from the street. "I don't need help," he said. Then, with the flicker of an apologetic smile—he'd been rude and now regretted it—he added, "But I'll help you when I come back."

After we got the garbage out, we went for coffee. We talked about what a jerk our landlord was and I told Phil about my job. When we got back to the building he asked me if I'd like to go up and see his paintings.

As I stepped across the threshold of Philip's attic apartment, I was conscious of entering a world where chaos was the rule; I glanced over my shoulder with a sense of bidding sweet reason goodbye. Phil leaned toward me as he pulled in the door, his expression mildly expectant, and I understood that he found nothing appalling in the broiling havoc of his domestic arrange-ments. The heat, freighted with turpentine fumes, assaulted me, as fierce as a roomful of tigers, but Philip brushed past me easily on his way to the air conditioner, an ancient rusty metal box perched on a rotted sill, the wall beneath it permanently stained by a bloom of mildew. It came on with a gasp, a metallic groan, and settled down to a roar. Philip turned to me, gesturing to the machine. "It doesn't work too good," he said. "And it leaks on the guy's balcony downstairs, so he gets pissed off when I run it."

"Tell him to put a plant under it," I suggested.

"That's not a bad idea," he said. "That's actually a good idea."

I had taken one, then another step into the room and could now be said to be inside it. Because the windows were all dormers, the light lay in thick swaths, leaving the rest in deep shadow. It was twice as big as my apartment, but there was half as much space. As my eyes adjusted to the combination of brightness and gloom, I saw that there was a pattern to the disorder. Everything having to do with painting was in the light, with living in the shadow. There was also a difference in the quality of unidentifiable stuff lining the walls; some was in piles, some in neat stacks.

Philip disappeared behind a wooden screen draped with clothing. "Would you like something to drink?"

"Just water," I said, advancing another step. Near the screen was a card table with two metal folding chairs which looked like a safe destination. The table was littered with newspapers, a plate of cigarette butts, a mug with coffee dregs in the bottom, and, incongruously, a bright orange satsuma. I took a seat facing the imposing easel in the brightest spot near the windows. There were canvases stacked about, only a few facing out. Their subjects were street scenes, buildings; there was a watercolor sketch of a stand of crepe myrtles that looked highly competent to me. The unfinished canvas on the easel was a moody study of rooftops.

Philip appeared with two glasses of tap water. "No ice," he said. "The freezer doesn't work."

I took the glass, nodding toward the window. "Those are good," I said. To my relief, Philip showed no artistic prickliness or vanity, no skepticism about my critical expertise. "That's the view from the roof," he said of the work in progress. "When it gets too hot at night I go out there."

We sat and talked. After a while Philip put a record on the

phonograph—it was the popular "After Bathing at Baxter's"—and I ate the satsuma. When the time came for me to leave for my shift, he escorted me downstairs to my apartment. On the staircase he rested a hand on my shoulder, in the shady patio he brushed my hair back with his fingertips, at the door he passed his arm around my waist and kissed me. It was a slow kiss, unlike any I had previously experienced, more tentative than exploratory, serious and courteous. "What time do you get off?" he said.

The venues for professional artists in our city were limited, and though I was not a student of the subject, I knew Philip didn't fit into any of them. He was not sufficiently avant-garde to show in the uptown galleries where there were openings with wine and cheese and where the buyers were called "clients," and the paintings "investments." He wasn't bad enough to please the tourists who fluttered along with the pigeons on Jackson Square, having their portraits done in chalk or dickering over the prices of ghastly renditions of patios and bizarre bayou scenes in which the sky was an unnatural shade of green. He might have done commercial art; he had the technical skill, but he disdained such employment. He had learned his craft at the Neil McMurtry School of Art, a private academy run by the eponymous painter who was occasionally commissioned to do large public works. I had whiled away many a Sunday morning in my childhood gazing up at four enormous toes which protruded from beneath the tablecloth at the Last Supper, part of an altar fresco executed by the esteemed McMurtry. The provenance of those toes was the subject of my earliest attempts at art appreciation. Were they attached to the Savior, or the fellow next to him? My parents seemed to think McMurtry was the Louisiana equivalent of Caravaggio, but Philip said his work was overrated. Still he recalled his time at the school with a romantic nostalgia. The sentence that began, "When we were at McMurtry's . . ." generally ended with a sigh. He had met Sid at McMurtry's; the standoff that was their friendship had begun there, when they were both promising.

I knew, everyone knew at a glance, that Philip was very poor but I believed, as I assumed he did, that this was a temporary condition. What money he had came from a small gallery on Decatur St. where the paintings were not so much displayed as crammed, often without frames, on every available inch of wall space. We were standing in this air-conditioned refuge one steaming afternoon in July when I first heard about Ingrid.

Philip was looking at a mawkish rendition of a sad clown, a woman wearing a white costume with puffy black pompoms for buttons, white face, red downturned mouth, pointy white hat. The background was solid red, the same shade as the mouth. I've never liked anything about clowns and this painting seemed designed to confirm my distaste. "This is Ingrid's," Phil said to the owner, Walter Stack, who looked up from a bin of canvases he was arranging according to size and said, "Sure."

"She still with Hazel?"

"Sure," Walter said. He returned his attention to the pictures.

Philip frowned at the frowning clown. "Hazel is all wrong for her," he said.

Walter abandoned the canvases and gave Philip a look I took to be sympathetic, though there was an edge of pity in it that made me anxious. He leaned a painting of a flowerpot—the paint was laid on like butter—against the counter, and, nodding at the heavy cardboard portfolio Philip had pressed against his side, said, "What have you got for me? More wallpaper?"

Philip lifted the portfolio to the counter and opened it

diffidently, his shoulders slumped forward in a way I had not seen before. He lacks confidence, I thought. "I have a few on the wallpaper," he said. "I'm finding that an interesting medium."

Walter began pulling out the various sheets, laying them side by side. "I sold the Beethoven," he said. "Do you have any more Beethoven?"

"Not this time," Philip said. "I could do another one."

"Do a few," Walter said. "I could sell maybe three or four."

"I can do that," Philip said. He turned to me, taking the small canvas he had wrapped in a pillowcase, which I held against my chest. He placed it carefully on the counter and pulled away the cloth. It was a painting of the rooftops outside his studio window. I thought it the best thing he had. Walter leaned over it skeptically, working his lips as if he were chewing something sour. "You see, I can't sell this," he said. "It could be anywhere. If you put the church in it, maybe. Tourists want stuff that says, 'This is New Orleans. I was there.' And they don't want anything dark. This is too dark."

Philip nodded, folding the pillowcase back over the canvas. I had the sense that this scene of crude rejection had taken place many times before; that he had, in fact, expected it, but it was new to me and it sickened me. "What about Beethoven?" I piped up, to my own surprise. "Beethoven doesn't say, 'This is New Orleans,' but you sold that."

Both men shifted their attention to me with the combination of interest and incredulity a cat might expect should it suddenly express an opinion. It pleased me to see that the balance in Philip's expression was weighted toward interest, whereas incredulity tipped the scales in Walter's alarmed and thorough regard. "Beethoven," he sputtered. "Beethoven says Beethoven. Everyone knows him, everyone loves him. He's like Einstein, or

Marilyn Monroe." He dismissed me with a wave of his fleshy hand, adding to Philip, "Bring me Einstein or Marilyn and I'll sell the pants off of 'em."

As we staggered out into the blinding light on the street, Philip mumbled, "I can do a few more Beethoven."

"Who is Ingrid?" I asked.

Ingrid was Philip's former girlfriend, who had shared an apartment with him—not the current attic but a larger space in a building close to Jackson Square. This was convenient as they were both doing portraits for tourists, pushing out their paint carts early in the morning, sharing the street with the horse carriages rather than risk the flood of refuse swirling across the sidewalks and the water curtains pouring off the balconies as the hose-bearing residents washed down their terrain in preparation for another sun-scorched day. It surprised me to learn that Philip had plied his art on the Square and he admitted that he had done it in desperation, and not for long, because he had no knack for pleasing tourists; they did not like his portraits or his person and haggled over the agreed-upon price or even refused to pay. "Ingrid is good at it," he said. "She has a real professional patter down. They eat it up."

"So she's still out there?"

"Sure," Philip says. "She has a license; the space right across from the Cabildo."

It didn't take much probing to learn that Ingrid, after two years of cohabitation during which, Philip confessed, they had "fought all the time," had left Philip for another woman, a bartender at the Anchor, a sleazy establishment frequented by divers. This was Hazel, who was, in Philip's view, "all wrong" for Ingrid. He was perfectly candid in his assessment of this failed relationship and seemed relieved to talk about it. I felt hardly a twinge of jealousy, but I was curious to see this woman who had rejected Phil, and, as it was easily done—I had only to alter my usual walk to the restaurant by a few blocks—the next morning I slipped from the alley into the cool shade of the Cabildo portico and, half hidden by a column, observed my predecessor in Phil's affections.

Or rather I observed her back, for she was facing the square, seated on a fold-up stool before her easel, her tray of pastels on a plastic cart next to her, one hand lazily conveying a cigarette back and forth between the tin ashtray on the shelf and her mouth. She wore a halter dress; her back, bony and tan, was bare. Her thick blonde hair, poorly cut and none too clean, fell about her shoulders in clumps. On her easel, hung on the iron fence, propped against plastic cartons on the pavement near her feet, were samples of her wares, garish pastel portraits of famous personalities, Barbra Streisand, Einstein, Mick Jagger, Sophia Loren. Her specialty was a bizarre twinkling in the eye and a Mona Lisa serenity at the corners of the mouth. The backgrounds were all the same, a hasty scrawl of sky-blue chalk. As I watched, three tourists, a young man and two teenage girls, paused to examine Barbra Streisand. The artist ignored them for one last drag on the cigarette, then stubbed it out in the ashtray and addressed a remark to the group. I couldn't hear what she said, but she had shifted on her stool, and I could see her profile, which was all planes and angles, the cheekbones jutting over deep hollows, the nose bladelike, the chin a sharp wedge of bone. Her eyes, like those of her celebrities, had a chilling glitter to them. The tourists were not dismayed; in fact they lingered for some moments talking to her. The taller of the girls laughed twice; the young man appeared fascinated and ill at ease. Were they considering a portrait?

As I watched this scene, it occurred to me that Ingrid had no idea who I was and that there was no necessity for stealth. I stepped out from behind my column and sat down on the wide step next to an elderly black man who was lovingly unpacking a saxophone. This square was the most public of spaces, designed in order that strangers might eye one another at their leisure. The tourists had evidently asked for directions. Ingrid raised her arm and pointed toward the river. After a brief exchange, they walked away, the taller girl looking back with a shy wave as they went. I got up and wandered toward the square, pausing to smile upon a child emptying a bag of popcorn over the bobbing heads of an aggressive flock of pigeons. I turned back at the gate to the square, pretending an interest in the facade of the cathedral.

This put me very close to Ingrid, who was occupied in lighting another cigarette. Clearly a heavy smoker. She had the pinched skin around the nose, the bloodless lips. Probably a serious drinker too, judging by the glassiness of her eyes, the slight tremor in her hands. I pictured her kissing Philip, but it was difficult; she was so coarse and she was several inches taller than he was. Two plumes of smoke issued from her nose. She's like some dreadful harpy, I thought. Waving the smoke away with one hand, she said clearly, "That's a nice skirt." Who was she talking to? I followed her eyes, which left the easel in front of her and turned with surprising force upon me, moving swiftly up from my skirt, over my waist, my breasts and to my astonished face. Her thin lips pulled back into a ghastly smile full of amusement at my discomposure, which was complete. I was so flummoxed I took a step backward and collided with the fence. "It fits you well," she added.

"Thanks," I said lamely, then recovered my footing and fled into the square. I didn't run, but I made directly for the opposite gate.

I crossed the street quickly and threw myself down at the furthest table in the Café du Monde.

So this was Ingrid.

Though I never actually saw Philip pick up a brush or pen, in the next week his apartment sprouted a crop of Beethoven. There he was glowering from behind a chair, propped atop a stack of books, face to face with himself across the kitchen table. Phil had gotten a new supply of wallpaper samples which were scattered about the easel, splayed open to his various selections. Sometimes, when we were having coffee, he hauled one of these books into his lap and thumbed through it as we talked. The samples provided the atmosphere of each portrait, swirling paisley, pointillist, pastoral; Philip worked the designs right into his subject's coat-sleeves and collar. But the face remained the same, instantly recognizable, the lunatic's thinning, unkempt hair, the overgrown brows, the pugilistic glare, the scowling lips, the brutish jaw, reminding his audience that this was the son of a drunken thug, the epitome of the Romantic, the scourge of the drawing room, the enemy of livery, the doom of the aristocracy, the death of manners.

"What is it you like about Beethoven?" I asked Phil one night when we were perched on his roof smoking cigarettes.

"The later quartets," he said. "Some of the symphonies. The Fifth, the Seventh, and the Ninth. Everybody likes those."

"No," I said. "Not the music. What is it about his face that you like?"

Phil considered my question. A mosquito landed on his arm and he brushed it off with the back of his hand. "It's easy to draw," he said.

As the summer burned on, I began to hate my job. I wasn't

good at it and my boss had noticed. I could never remember who had ordered what and I could only carry two cups of coffee at a time, whereas Betty, who had worked there for years, could carry four. Once I set a tray of sandwiches and drinks down on a portable serving table and the whole thing tipped over onto the floor. I sometimes forgot to squirt the ersatz whipped cream on the bread pudding. If the diners were impatient or rude, as, because of my ineptitude, they often were, I became sullen. I worked for tips, we all did, and I wasn't doing very well.

One night, after a particularly miserable shift during which I had knocked over a water glass while serving a bowl of gumbo to a miserly spinster, a regular who disliked me, Phil and I were sitting on his roof batting our hands at the humid, bug-laden air and drinking lukewarm beer. I complained about my job, about my boss and the harridans in the kitchen, about my dislike of the customers and my refusal to curry favor to get bigger tips. "It doesn't work anyway," I said. "They know I'm faking it and they hate me for it."

"You should never fake it," he said. "If you can't be authentic doing whatever you're doing, you should do something else."

"I'm sure that's true," I said, though I wasn't sure at all. "But this is the job I have."

"You should read Sartre," he said. "Inauthenticity is a fatal disease. It kills you, one day at a time."

"So you think I should quit my job."

"The option is to take it seriously, engage in it, become it, while you're a waitress, become a waitress and nothing else."

This was the first and probably the only advice Phil ever gave me. I drank my beer and mulled it over. It didn't occur to me that Phil was unlikely to be the source of a recipe for successful living, and there was something in his formula—be engaged or be damned—that struck me as eminently reasonable. It still does. I had not, until that moment, identified myself simply as what I was, a waitress, and not a very good one. "It's not easy," I said, meaning my job.

"It's odd, isn't it?" Phil said. "You'd think it would be hard to fake it, but evidently it isn't." He held out his hand to the rooftops spread like open books all around us. "Sometimes when I sit out here," he said, "I think about what's really going on under every one of these roofs. That's the reason I like to paint this view, it's the lid of the problem. Look how close together they are. It wouldn't take much to burn the whole Quarter down; it's happened before." He extracted a cigarette from the pack in his shirt pocket, his lighter from his pants. "There's a flashpoint down there somewhere. Sometimes I think if I just dropped a match in the right place . . ." He lit the cigarette and exhaled a mouthful of smoke. I considered the vision, flames leaping from the windows, bursting through the rooftops, the screams of the desperate residents clinging to the rickety staircases, jumping from their wrought-iron balconies to the stone courtyards below.

"Then you'd see some authentic behavior," Phil concluded.

I tried taking Phil's advice but my efforts to become a waitress only made me more disgusted with myself at the end of my shift when I counted out the paltry bills in my apron pocket. Phil was poor too, but at least he was doing what he wanted to do. Except for the weekly visits to my family, I spent my spare time with him, and I was comfortable with him as I had never been with the high-spirited college boys who were like thoughtless children spinning about in circles on the lawn, intent on disorienting their senses. Phil was frugal, modest, and he seemed to personally like me. When I arrived at his door, he was genuinely pleased by the sight of me. When we went out together he was attentive; his eyes did not wander the room looking for something more interesting.

Walter Stack took five of the Beethoven and in the next few weeks he sold three, which constituted a windfall for Philip. He was relieved to have the money; it was enough to pay his back rent and splurge on a bottle of wine which we drank with the undercooked chicken cacciatore I whipped up in my gloomy kitchen, but something about this very limited success made Phil irritable and anxious. The fact that only three had sold was evidence that he need do no more, the craze was over. However, if the two remaining sold, as Walter expected they would, then he would be condemned to produce more, and the truth was, he was already sick of Beethoven. If he wasn't careful he would be the guy who did Beethoven, which evidently struck him as an appalling fate.

"You don't have to do nothing but Beethoven," I protested. "Beethoven could be a sideline."

"I'm not a printmaker," Phil snapped. "I don't do editions. Every painting is different. It has to be. One leads to the other."

"Didn't Monet do a lot of waterlilies?" I suggested hopefully. "And a series of Chartres Cathedral too. That was the same subject over and over."

Phil gave me a guarded look, which encouraged me. "Don't artists always do a lot of studies before they finish a big project? Maybe all the Beethovens are just the warm-up for the big one."

Phil drained his glass and poured out another full one. "That's ridiculous," he said.

"You like to paint the rooftops again and again," I persisted. "You've said yourself you don't tire of that."

"Well, that's the point, isn't it," he said. "Every time I look out the window it's different. The light has changed; it's cloudy or clear, or raining. It's alive. Beethoven is dead."

That shut me up. I pushed the chicken around with my fork, sipped my wine, keeping my eyes down.

"And I'm not Monet." He said this resignedly, as if he didn't want to hurt my feelings.

I've never been much interested, as some women are, in trying to make something out of a man, in seeing his promise and compelling him to live up to it. I figured Phil was an artist and I wasn't, so he probably knew more about being one than I did. Everyone agreed that artists were, by their nature, difficult people. Maybe Phil's problem was that he wasn't difficult enough. He certainly wasn't egotistical, but he was stubborn. He did no more Beethoven that summer, and I said nothing more about it. He started doing self-portraits on the wallpaper samples, choosing some of the ugliest designs in the books, dark swirls and metallic stripes, paper for a child's room with romping pink elephants chasing beach balls. There was something sinister about these pictures. The likeness was good, but the eyes were wrong, unfocused and as lightless as a blind man's. As soon as they were done, Phil put them away in an old cardboard portfolio.

One evening when we were drinking beer with Sid and Wendy, Sid asked Phil what he was working on. "I'm in transition," Phil said. This answer struck me as unnecessarily vague; it wasn't as if Phil was not working. "He's doing self-portraits," I said. Sid stroked his well-kept beard, an irritating habit he had. "On the wallpaper," he said. "Sure," Phil said. I started turning my coaster around on the table, waiting for Sid's pronouncement, which would provoke the usual argument, but Sid said nothing. When I looked up he was signaling the waitress. "I'll buy a round," he said.

Phil drained the glass he'd been lingering over, his eyes fixed coldly on Sid's back. If Sid was buying, it meant we were in for a lecture.

"Thanks," I said to Wendy, who smiled.

"We're celebrating," she said. "We have good news."

Sid turned to us, his face radiating self-importance, but he left it to Wendy to satisfy our curiosity.

"Sid's taken a job at Dave Gravier's agency."

Even I had heard of the Gravier agency, which had produced the stylish Jazz and Crawfish festival posters that hung in upscale restaurants and shops all over town. "That's great," I said.

"It's just part time," Sid said.

Phil fumbled a cigarette from his pack, his mouth fixed in a lopsided smile. The waitress arrived with our beers and a basket of tortilla chips, which Sid pulled closer to himself.

"So you sold out," Phil said softly.

Sid took a chip, bit it, chewing ruminatively as he rolled his eyes heavenward.

"And I knew you would," Phil added.

Sid swallowed his chip, while Wendy and I exchanged speculative glances. "It's just part time," Sid repeated.

"For now," Phil said.

"No, not just for now, Philip," Sid insisted. "I made it very clear to Dave that I am only willing to work for him three days a week because I'm planning a new series of paintings, large canvases, bigger than anything I've done before, and they'll be expensive to produce. So I'm willing to work part time in order to increase my creative options, not, as you imply, to limit them, which means I'm not selling out. It's the opposite of selling out. I'm interested in doing important work, lasting work, and I can't do that by painting on grocery bags or feed sacks, or linoleum tiles I pull up from the kitchen floor. I need canvas and lots of it, big, sturdy frames, a lot of paint, and that stuff, as you may not know these days, my friend, because you are living in a dream, is expensive."

"Tell yourself that lie," Phil said, giving me a sidelong glance that presupposed my agreement.

"No," I said. "I see your point."

"An artist has to live in the real world," Sid informed us.

"Right," Phil snapped, stubbing his cigarette out in the ashtray. "And the real world has got to be a lot more comfortable than the one I'm living in. Which is what, would you say, some kind of anti-reality? A counter-world?"

"Money is freedom," Sid replied, ignoring, I thought, Phil's excellent point, which was that everything is reality, suffering, success, poverty, wealth, a rat-infested hovel or a mansion; it's all the same stuff. "And I need freedom to work, I'm not stymied. I'm not making excuses for myself, I'm not 'In transition,' I'm not afraid to work and I'm not selling out to the establishment. I'm grateful for the establishment. I need money, and now I won't have to worry about getting it and I can work in peace."

We were all quiet for a moment, listening to the fact that Sid had used Phil's expression "in transition" as the locus of his general contempt. I expected Phil to fire back forcefully, but he just swallowed half of his beer, set the glass down carefully and said, "You're just clueless, Sid."

On the walk home, Phil was quiet. I chattered on about my visit with my parents, who were pressing me to go back to school, my dissatisfaction with my job, the roach problem in my kitchen, which boric acid wasn't touching. We trudged up the stairs to Phil's apartment where the heat was packed in so tight it hurt to breathe. "For God's sake," I said, "turn on the air conditioner."

"It's broken," he said.

I leaned against the table feeling my pores flush out across my forehead and back. "When did that happen?"

"This morning." Phil had stripped his shirt off and was bending over a stack of wallpaper sample books.

"We can't stay here," I said. "Let's go to my place. At least I have a fan."

"You go," he said pleasantly. "There's something I need to do here."

"Are you going to paint?"

He gathered up a few of the sample books and carried them, weaving slightly, to the kitchen table. Then he pulled one of the jumbo garbage bags from the roll under the sink. "I'm getting rid of these," he said.

"Tonight?" I said. "Can't it wait until tomorrow?"

"No," he said.

I took up a dish towel and wiped it across my forehead. "It's too hot, Phil," I complained. "And I'm too tired."

"I don't need help," he said. "Just go to bed. I'll see you in the morning."

The thought of the comfortable bed in my clammy room off the alley was appealing. I rarely slept there because it was too narrow for both of us. The sheets were clean; the tick-tick of the oscillating fan always reminded me of sleeping at my grandmother's house when I was a child. "I'm going," I said.

Phil scarcely looked up from the bagging of the sample books. "Goodnight," he said. "Sleep well."

A few days later Phil and I stopped by Walter Stack's gallery to see if the remaining Beethoven had sold. Phil had nothing new to offer; as far as I could tell he had stopped painting and he was running out of money. "What is this? You're coming here empty-handed?" Walter complained as soon as we were inside the door.

"I'm working," Phil replied. "I'll have something in a few days."

I scanned the crowded walls and spotted Beethoven scowling out beneath a charcoal rendering of Charlie Chaplin. The famous-dead area, I presumed.

"I was wondering if you'd sold any of the Beethoven," Phil asked. Something in Walter brought out a diffidence in Phil that made my stomach turn.

"I did sell one," Walter said. "A lady from Oregon who plays the piano." He turned to the cash register and punched the buttons until the drawer sprang open. I smiled at Phil; surely this was good news, but he was looking past me, out at the street, with an expression of such excitement mixed with fear that I turned to see what he saw. Two women were maneuvering an oversized port-folio through the heavy glass door. The one at the back was a tall, muscular redhead, the other, pushing in determinedly, was Ingrid.

"Look," Walter said. "Now here's a working artist. What have you got for me, beautiful?"

Ingrid's hawkish eyes raked the room, drawing a bead on Phil who was pocketing the single bill Walter had pulled from the register. "Hi, Phil," she said, pleasantly enough.

"Hello, Ingrid," Phil replied. He stepped away from the coun-ter, close to me, and I assumed he was about to introduce me. Having cleared the door the two women passed us and lifted the portfolio to the counter. While Ingrid unfastened the ribbons along the side, her friend engaged Walter in light banter about another dealer. I craned my neck, hoping to get a look at Ingrid's offering, but the counter was narrow and she was forced to hold the cover upright, blocking my view. Walter looked down doubt-fully at whatever was displayed, working his jaw. I turned to Phil, thinking he must be as curious as I was.

He was leaning away from me, his weight all on one leg, his shoulders oddly hunched, and as I watched, he raised one hand and pressed the knuckle lightly against his lips. The color had drained from his face and he swayed as if he might collapse, yet there was a vibration of energy around him, a kind of heat. His dark eyes were fixed with a febrile intensity on Ingrid's back, bathing her with such a combination of sweetness, longing, and terror that I thought she must feel it. Or hear it. Indeed his expression aroused in me sensations similar to those evoked by the commencement of certain melancholy music, a shiver along the spine, the silencing of the inner colloquy, all the senses arrested by an unwelcome yet irresistible revelation of suffering.

Ingrid didn't feel it. She was engaged in bargaining, which was pointless as Walter took everything on consignment and set the prices himself. Her friend brought up the other dealer again, suggesting that he would make a better offer, and Walter, obligingly, pretended outrage. Phil's hand had dropped to his side, but otherwise he didn't move. He was so rapt in his contemplation of Ingrid, so unconscious of everything else, including me, that when I touched his arm it startled him and he gripped my hand tightly. "Phil," I said. "Let's go now," and I led him, unprotesting, into the street. The group at the counter, absorbed in their transactions, took no notice of our departure.

Outside the light and heat assailed us and we clung to each other until we reached the covered sidewalk on Decatur St. "Do you want to go for a coffee?" I asked, and Phil nodded. His eyes were wet, but his color had returned and he gave me a weak, convalescent smile. "We'll go inside," he said. "It will be cool in there."

That night we brought my fan up to Phil's apartment, but it was still too hot to sleep. I tossed and turned. Phil left my side without speaking and climbed out the window to smoke a cigarette on the roof. Anxiety was my bedfellow, a many-headed hydra snapping at me with undisguised fury. My future unfolded before me, a black hole of thankless, boring work. What are you going to do? I asked myself repeatedly, urgently. At length I got up and went to the kitchen. The moon was full, there was a shaft of creamy white across the ugly floor, lighting my way to the refrigerator. I poured a glass of water and sat naked at the kitchen table, looking about in a panic. There was more room without the wallpaper books, and Phil had cleared off his easel, which struck me as suspicious and portentous. What would happen next? What was Phil going to paint on now? Doubtless Sid was right and Phil had been using the wallpaper, not for the interesting creative possibilities it afforded, but because the books were free and he couldn't afford canvas, or even cheap board. My eyes rested on the mottled linoleum at my feet. Would Phil take Sid's suggestion and start prying the tiles up off the floor?

This thought cast me down very low. I had left school because I wanted to live in the real world and now I was doing just that and I didn't like it at all. My childish fantasy of an untroubled and companionable relationship with a man who valued me was clearly the worst sort of naiveté, though oddly enough I'd gotten what I wanted. Phil was easy, kind, and I did not doubt that he cared for me. But in the gallery that day I had seen him unmanned by an unrequited and impossible passion for a woman who cared nothing for him. It wasn't his weakness that had shocked me; it was the invincibility of his ardor, which clearly could brook no dissembling, even in public, even in front of me. To be either the subject or the object of such a humiliating, destructive force was not a condition I could ever tolerate. "There's just no future in it," I said to myself, purposefully vague about the pronoun reference. Was "it" my life with Phil? Or was "it" the whole catastrophic enterprise of romantic love?

Eventually Phil climbed back in the window and found me there, naked, clutching my water glass and staring into the blackness between us. He went to the refrigerator and looked inside. "I've got a cold beer we could split," he said.

"That sounds good," I said.

He brought the beer to the table and sat down across from me, opening the can with a can opener. I finished my water and held out the glass for my share.

"You can't sleep," Phil observed.

"It's too hot," I said.

"Do you want to go out?"

"No."

"OK," Phil said. We sipped our beer.

"I just don't see what you're going to do now," I said.

"What do you mean?"

"Well, with the self-portraits, and no more wallpaper and no more Beethoven. I don't see how you'll make a living."

"I'll think of something," he said.

"Maybe Sid has the right idea. You could get some part-time work. That might take the pressure off."

He smiled. "I don't want to take the pressure off," he said. "The pressure is part of it."

"Part of what?" I said. "Being miserable?"

"I'm not miserable."

I considered this.

"But you are," he said.

"I hate my job," I said.

"Then you should quit."

"And do what?"

For answer, Phil finished his beer, got up and took the empty can to the sink. He came behind me and began rubbing my shoulders. "You're very tense," he said.

I let myself go limp beneath his hands. "I know," I said. He worked my neck between his fingers and his palm, up and down until I let my head fall back against his chest. He leaned down to kiss me languidly. "Is it too hot to do this?" he asked, sliding his hand around my back and over my breast.

"No," I said. "I want to." Then, as I followed him to the rumpled mattress, I felt, in spite of everything, of the heat, of my disillusionment and frustration, of my fear of the future in which, we both knew, Phil would no longer figure, a perverse but unmistakable throb of dark desire.

THE UNFINISHED NOVEL

"Rita's back," Malcolm said. We were drinking iced coffee at a café on Esplanade, watching the traffic ooze through the heat haze. "She's living near here."

Rita. My God, Rita. She came at me from the past, from that first winter in Vermont, her thin woolen coat blowing open over a short cotton skirt, bare legs, picking her way across a snow bank in her high-heeled open-toed shoes. She won't last a year, I thought then, and I was right.

"Is she alone?" I asked.

"Oh, I think so. She's changed a lot. I didn't recognize her."

"In what way?"

"She's gained a lot of weight. She looks pasty, not healthy."

This surprised me. Rita had been thin, willowy, long-limbed, big hands, boyish hips.

"What's she doing?"

"It's hard to tell. She was pretty vague. She wanted me to believe she was involved in some top-secret mission for the Pueblo Indians."

"Wow," I said. The waiter appeared with our check, which I snatched away from Malcolm.

"Thanks," he said.

"My pleasure."

"You haven't changed," he observed.

I come back to New Orleans every few years and stay only long enough to convince myself it's time to leave, which takes between two weeks and three months. Whenever I return, my friends are always quick to observe that I haven't changed, which I take to mean I still have most of my hair. Malcolm, who once sported a full crop of coarse black thatch, has lost most of it, save a monkish tonsure he has the good sense to trim close. He has a well-kept beard, compensation for what's gone on top, and he's developed the beard-stroking habit, which annoys me. As a young man he was dissolute, a womanizer, heavy drinker, chain-smoker, not promising, but to everyone's surprise including his own, he prospered. He has a successful furniture business, a devoted wife, several children, an expensive car and a large, tastefully appointed house near City Park. Having never read a novel, he has no opinion about the ones I've written, and, as he has no curiosity about my private life, his success has allowed us to remain friends. He neither resents nor envies me.

I paid the bill while Malcolm swatted at a fly grazing on the remains of his brioche. "She asked about you," he said.

"What did she want to know?"

"If I was in touch with you. If I knew where you were."

"I hope you didn't tell her."

"Well, I did. But you're bound to run into her sooner or later, so it doesn't matter. If women want to find you, they always know how to go about it."

"How much weight would you say she's gained?" I asked.

"A lot," Malcolm laughed. "But she still has beautiful hair."

Not a week passed before I walked into the post office and got in line behind Rita Richard. I didn't recognize her. What I saw was the wide back of an overweight woman, not a sight to provoke my interest, but there was something about this one that seemed familiar. Her curling, golden hair resisted the confines of an oversized clip. A cheap flowered blouse, stretched tight across her shoulders, was tucked haphazardly into the straining waistband of a differently flowered, voluminous skirt. Her ankles bulged around the thin straps of cruel, high-heeled sandals. Perhaps it was the shoes. Did some molecule floating around in my brain remember caressing those ankles, long ago, when there was a tantalizing space between the strap and the smooth bone of the instep? Whatever it was, I knew it was Rita, and my first instinct—if only I had succeeded in following it—was flight. I took a few cautious steps backward; at the same moment the line moved forward and a teenager who had just come in, his view obscured by the large package he intended to entrust to the US mail, collided with me. The ensuing apologies, excuses, and reassurances naturally engaged the attention of everyone in the place. As I helped the boy regain control of his package, I was aware that Rita had turned to see what the fuss was about, that she had recognized me, and that she was waiting for the matter to be settled, which, no matter how I tried to extend it, was quickly accomplished. The boy went ahead; Rita stepped behind, smiling at me confidently. I was at pains to disguise a complex of emotions: consternation, shock, anxiety, and through it all the pang of recognition: this unappealing creature was certainly Rita, but how altered!

"Hello, Maxwell," Rita said. "I heard you were in town."

"Rita?" I said. "Is it really you? I thought you'd gone out West and become a stranger."

She laughed at this weak joke, and it was Rita's laugh, knowing, intimate, flirtatious. "I did," she said. "But now I'm back."

"How amazing to run into you," I faltered.

"Not really," she said. "It's a small town. Sooner or later we all come back."

"But to stay? Are you here to stay?"

"Oh, yes. I won't be leaving again. What about you?"

"It's just a visit for me."

"Of course. You're too famous to live here."

This was the kind of dismissive remark I get a lot in my hometown. I'm not famous, by any means, but I have a small reputation, or so I flatter myself, and I am able to live in modest comfort on the proceeds of my books. "Oh, I'm not famous," I said, but Rita wasn't interested in my answer. From somewhere within her skirt she had produced a purse, much too small for a woman her size, and she proceeded to dig in it, talking all the while, until she pulled out a battered checkbook from which she tore off a page. "I live a few blocks from here, on St. Ann," she said. "Here's the address. I'd like to talk to you about something; it's a sort of proposition." Here she gave me her raised eyebrows, compressed lips expression, suggesting the stifling of a naughty thought. "A business proposition. Will you come see me? Here's the address."

She held out the paper, which I eyed warily. "It's a deposit slip," she said. "It has my address on it. If you don't want to come see me, you can just make a deposit."

And be done with it, I thought. If only it were that simple. I took the flimsy paper; I couldn't see any way not to.

"It's not far from here," she said again.

"I suppose I could come by," I said.

She brought her hand up to her neck, pulling her fingers through the curls that were loose there, her light eyes fixed on me. It was a gesture so familiar and, in the new context, so perverse, it unsettled my reason. I had the sense that this woman was an impostor, that she had studied Rita, the real Rita, who was at that moment perfectly alive in my memory, as palpable as my own tongue in my mouth.

"How about tomorrow?" she said.

"No, I've got appointments all day." This was, in fact, true.

"Thursday?" Now she was amused, watching me squirm. I decided to limit her pleasure and my own suffering. "Thursday would be fine," I said. "In the afternoon, around three."

"I'll be there," she said.

Yes, I thought. I don't doubt you are there most of the time. "I'll see you then," I said, consulting my watch.

She looked concerned. "Don't you want to mail your letter, Maxwell?"

I gestured at the line, which was now down to one. Rita stepped aside, suggesting that she would generously yield her place to my urgent necessity, but I had only one thought and that was to terminate this interview. "I'll do it later," I said, and I fled like one pursued. Indeed, Rita did pursue me. As I was pulling out of the parking lot, I saw her standing at the plate-glass window, watching me stolidly as I drove away.

Among the dark strands of my dismay at having been so smoothly apprehended by Rita was a glittering thread of vindicated spite, for she had once made me very unhappy. I gloated over the details of her appearance, her run-down shoes, the missing top button of her blouse, her general air of shabbiness, failure. I had done well, and Rita decidedly had not. Who would have predicted such an outcome twenty years ago, on a certain freezing night in Vermont, when I shadowed Rita along a wind-swept alley, desperate to stop her from going in at a certain door?

*

I'd first met Rita in college. She was a year behind me; perhaps we had a class together, but she was not part of my group. She passed as an exotic when she got to Vermont, but in our sultry, provincial hometown she was just another tall, pretty waitress who slept around, drank too much and never stopped smoking. She was rumored to write poetry and once, at an open reading, I'd seen her read half a dozen perfectly forgettable lines, pausing to take a drag on a cigarette midway through. I had a girlfriend, the winsome Rachel Paige, who was entirely devoted to me and to my burning ambition to leave New Orleans and become a writer. It wasn't until I got my acceptance to the graduate writing program in Vermont that Rachel realized she had courteously helped me right out of her life, but to her credit, she was not resentful. Perhaps, by then, she was sick of me. I spent the summer before I left working as a bartender and pointing out to anyone in earshot that I couldn't wait to leave town. My conversation was tiresome. I hated the whole gestalt of the Southern storyteller, the home-spun crank who populated his stories with characters named Joleen, Angina, and Bubba-Joe-Henry, all of whom drove pickup trucks, drank Dixie beer, and knew everything there was to know about pigs. I was eager to shrug off my Southernness like a reptile's skin and ascend to the realms of transcendental bliss. I intoxicated myself reading Emerson and Thoreau; I wanted what they had, all of it, the self-reliance, the days as Gods, the different drummer, the excitement about ideas, the passionate love of nature, of writing, and of books. I wanted to write with the force Thoreau, reading Aeschylus, called "naked speech, the standing aside of words to make room for thoughts." I affirmed with Emerson the maxim that "our thoughts *are* our lives." Southerners, in my view, substituted stories for ideas and it was to me like offering marshmallow to a starving tiger. I was sick of it.

Of course, when I got to Vermont, I settled down and wrote stories like everyone else. Even if "naked speech" had been within my capabilities, it wasn't likely to sell, and I was, above all, a realist about the requirements of the market. But my characters had names like Winston and Edna, they worked at bookstores, they concerned themselves with ethical questions. By my second year, their inquiries were impeded by blizzards or locals who spoke in monosyllables. I let my beard grow out, discovered the virtues of flannel shirts, wool socks, lined rubber boots. My accent, never strong, faded; my hands were chapped. I enjoyed the not inconsequential pleasures of chopping wood. I had left the South behind, purposefully and finally, and I rejoiced in my new identity.

This was why I experienced a shudder down to my duck boots when, on the first day of the spring semester—which was a long, long way from spring—I walked into my workshop classroom to find Rita Richard bent over in her chair, trying to dry her feet with a handkerchief. She looked up at me through a flutter of thickly painted eyelashes and said, "Are you surprised to see me, Maxwell?"

I was so thoroughly taken aback that my response was an unchivalrous "What are you doing here?"

Rita finished her foot care and pulled her shoes back on with a grimace. Brendan Graves, with whom I drank beer most weekends, shot me a look of exaggerated inquiry. Did I know this singular creature? "I'm in the program," Rita said. "I applied too late for fall, so they let me come in now."

"I didn't know you wrote," I said.

"Well, I don't talk about it. But I do."

Our conversation was interrupted by the arrival of our professor, a writer of small reputation who is probably still laboring in the merciless groves of academe. I excused myself and took my seat across the table from Rita, next to Brendan, who quickly wrote *Who is she??* on his notebook and pushed it toward me.

From New Orleans, I wrote back. *An acquaintance, no more.*

Before the professor had finished the roll-call, everyone in the class had this information. Rita's Southern shtick was on full display. When he called her name, she lifted her palm and pulled her head back as if he'd offered her something distasteful. "It's Ree-shard," she said. He nodded, tried it, came out with "Ray-chard" and she corrected him, sweetly, patiently, until he got it right. "I'm from New Orleans," she said. "That's how we say it there, but only if it's your family name."

He paused, giving her a long look over the tops of his reading glasses. He was a handsome man, weathered, lots of curly gray hair, tweedy jacket over a sweater embroidered with cat fur. "New Orleans," he said. "You're a long way from home."

"I am just a little anxious about the snow," she said with a chirpy insouciance that sent a chuckle rippling around the table. "I wish I could just grow a beard, like Maxwell has." All eyes turned briefly upon me. In that moment, I hated Rita.

"That's right," the professor said. "You're from New Orleans too, aren't you, Max? I'd forgotten. And you two know each other?"

"Yes," Rita said. "Maxwell and I go way back."

"It's Max, Rita," I said. "Not Maxwell. Just Max."

Rita laughed. "Will I have to change my name too?"

"Well," the professor said. "You'll have to work that out with Max." He cast me the nervous smile of a man who avoids even the outskirts of a quarrel and continued the roll-call.

That spring, every Tuesday from four until six-thirty, I sat across the table from Rita in a steadily intensifying state of mystification. After the first day my expectations were naturally minimal. I was prepared to spend my time in class alternating between outrage and humiliation. I was determined to keep my distance from her. The first discussions in these venues are necessarily tentative and anxious, the air laden with portentous questions: is the professor competent, hostile, does someone talk too much or not at all, is there a peer whose writing one actively despises, do we take a break, is coffee allowed, is the room over- or underheated? There were eight of us, so it was not until the fifth meeting that we had each exhibited our wares and established a pecking order. Rita's turn came up at the end of the first rotation, by which time most of us had been treated to her personal critique. She invariably began with some specious disclaimer: "Now I know this isn't mine, but if it were," or "I may have gotten too *involved* in this story," after which she laid out her argument with the confidence of a general presenting a foolproof strategy for battle. Her recommendations were original and intuitive; she was able to enter into the writer's intentions with an open, inquisitive mind. My initial relief at not having to take issue with her every week gave way to admiration; she really had the requisite knack. It was clear that she read every piece several times. When we passed in the manuscripts to the author at the end of the class, I noticed hers were copiously annotated, her comments neatly printed in the margins in purple ink. By the time my own story came up for review, I was as eager to hear Rita's reaction as the professor's. Of course, though I had found her to be critically acute about the efforts of our peers, I didn't think Rita's remarks about my work were particularly useful. She made a few suggestions for structural changes that, if not improvements, presented provocative options. She observed, as others have over the years, that my female characters were shallow, lacking complexity and dimension. She said this with a laugh that made the professor inquire whether, in her opinion, this vacuity presented a serious problem. "No," she said. "I don't think it matters at all. In fact, I think it's intentional, at least I hope it is." Here she gave me her faux-naïf smile. "It mirrors forth the myopia of the narrator, doesn't it?"

Twenty years have passed and I can reproduce that sentence exactly as I heard it. I can still feel the soft osculation of Rita's voice, the full two syllables she gave to the word "mirrors," as she swept back the ever encroaching mass of her curls and raised her eyes to mine. Ostensibly she was giving me credit for having created a contemptible persona, but the coolness of her eyes on my suddenly burning cheeks left me with the sensation of having been rendered pitifully transparent. I looked away, at my own hands, at the table, at the professor, who studied the open pages of my manuscript, compressing his lips to contain a smile. Just you wait, I thought.

That very evening I carried to my chilly apartment the first thirty pages of Rita's work-in-progress, a novel, or, as she put it, "maybe a novel?" I made a cup of coffee and sat down at the desk, uncapping my red pen, intent on vengeance. An hour later I laid the pen across the unmarked pages and rested my head in my hands.

St. Ann is a long street that runs from the French Quarter all the way to Bayou St. John. On either end, near the river and near the park, it's respectable enough, but there is a stretch that curves around a derelict canning factory that is decidedly unsavory. As I followed the numbers descending into this area, I was increasingly conscious of my car, a late model Volvo, which announced to the loitering residents the status of its owner as an alien, possibly a landlord. Because I had to keep one eye out for the house numbers and the other on the minefield of potholes in the road, some so deep the wheel sank in to the hubcap, my progress was slow.

The houses were all rickety structures, single or double shotguns, raised on chunky brick piers, sagging in various directions, all in need of paint. Some of the porches were packed with junk, a few sported melancholy potted plants or plastic garden chairs. The sidewalk undulated over tree roots, cracked in places and sprouting fierce patches of weeds. Erosion had worn away the edges of the road, leaving a ditch in which all parking was on an angle. I spotted the correct number, four iron digits nailed into the porch column of a house as shabby as its neighbors, and guided the Volvo cautiously into the ditch. A worn-out man in an undershirt, sitting on the front step of the neighboring house, got up and went inside. From a narrow alley between his house and Rita's, a cat came stealthily toward my car.

I got out and stood gazing at the house front. Rita's porch was bare. One side was obscured and softened by the bright green curtain of a plantain tree, and there was a vine curling in the rails, some adventitious weed intent on destruction. On a neighboring porch a huddle of teenagers shouted at one another in their secret language, doubtless making plans to flatten my tires or scratch the paint with a broken bottle, such as the one glinting in the ditch at my feet. I pressed the remote device in my pocket and the car emitted a brief yelp and click as the locks closed down. The cat let out a screech which sounded dire, though it didn't move from its station on the sidewalk.

I like cats, so I walked around the car to speak to this one. As I approached the animal slunk away, but I determined that it was in poor condition, spectrally thin, with a sparse coat and ears so infected by mites they were malformed. I'd had the air conditioning on in the car and the heat enveloped me, closing over my face like a hot iron mask, so severe and sudden I gasped for breath. I could see that Rita's door was open behind the screen, which meant there was no air conditioning. I scanned the side for a window unit; maybe she only cooled one room, but there was nothing. How does anyone live in this heat? I thought. Then, from under Rita's porch, from the plantain's grove of stems, from beneath a dust-clad azalea in the neighbor's yard, from the alley of the house next door, from the open window of the rusted Dodge Dart corroding in the ditch behind my Volvo, there issued a legion of cats.

They didn't press me, they didn't even approach, but their intention was clearly to appraise me, to determine whether I might be, in any sense, a potential source of food. Their collective gaze was chilling. If our respective sizes had been reversed, I would have stood in fear for my life. I looked from one to the other; they were uniformly thin and scant of coat; every one of them had the encrusted deformed ears that denote severe infection. I resisted an impulse to get back in the car, drive to the nearest vet, and purchase a gallon of ear-mite cream and a dozen hav-a-heart traps. Hostility toward the human residents of this street animated me. Of course they were all poor, but couldn't they see this suffering in their midst and organize to do something about it? Wasn't there one among them who sympathized with these luckless scavengers, which surely provided them the service of keeping their vicinity rat-free?

Rita, for example. I cast an accusing eye at her door. She was standing there in the semi-darkness behind the screen, looking back at me. *She's* certainly getting enough to eat, I thought, and I scowled at her as she pushed the door open and stepped out into the light.

"Hello, Maxwell," she said. "I thought you might not come."

At the sound of the screen door the cats scattered. "Something should be done about these cats," I said, going up the cement steps to her porch. "They've all got ear infections."

"They're feral cats," she observed. "You could never catch them."

"At least the SPCA could be notified," I insisted. "The cats in Rome are in better shape than these."

"Are they?" Rita said, without interest.

I was about to extol the virtues of the Roman cat association, which cares for the feline populations of various public areas, but before I'd begun, I looked at Rita, who so impossibly filled the doorway, and the shock of her transformation struck me anew. I searched for some dissembling remark. "It's very hot," I said.

"It's a little better inside." She stepped back, opening the screen door, and I looked past her into the house. When my eyes adjusted to the gloom, I realized I was looking into her bedroom. I was fixed between curiosity and foreboding, and stymied by the unsettling feeling of having done this before. It wasn't déjà vu, it was an actual memory: Rita, the real Rita, with her slender wrists and light, penetrating eyes, opening another door while I hesitated, stamping snow from my boots. "For God's sake, Maxwell," she was saying. "Come on in. You know you're dying to." As I had then, I summoned my courage and stepped inside. Rita came in behind me, pausing to latch the screen. "Go on through to the kitchen," she said. "There's a fan in there."

The shotgun house, so named because a rifle fired at the front door can hit a target, presumably fleeing for his life, on the back porch, is a singularly ungracious yet practical architectural development. The rooms are lined up with central doors opening from one to the other; the kitchen is always at the back. They are comprised of from two to six rooms; most have four; Rita had three. My impression of the place, as I made for the promised fan, was of disorder and penury. The bed was a double—Rita would need the space—pushed into a corner, gray sheets rumpled, the single pillow afloat near the center. There was a chipped table pushed up against the metal footboard, on which a small television perched amid heterogeneous stacks that included books, dishes, and bags of chips. The next room was furnished with tables, though none for dining. They were pushed into the four corners, and piled with more junk. Some of it was pottery of a brickish hue, much of it broken. As in the front room, the shades were drawn, the air stifling. There wasn't a chair in sight. The kitchen, while not welcoming, was a relief. A ceiling fan whirred overhead, churning the oppressive air. The back door was open, letting in a block of softened light. This room had wooden shutters which were partly opened and latched, admitting the light in muted slashes. The furnishings were minimal, the appliances venerable, the countertops covered in chipped red linoleum, as was the floor; everything was clear and clean. In the center of the room a porcelain-topped table and two sturdy white chairs suggested the possibility of a tête-à-tête.

Rita followed me, taking down two plastic glasses from a shelf as I sat at the table. "Would you like some lemonade?" she asked.

"I would, yes," I said.

She opened the refrigerator and I had a view of the largely empty shelves. She took out a plastic pitcher and set it on the table with the glasses. "So, Maxwell, how long will you be in town?" she said.

"Not long," I replied. "It's too hot."

She poured out two glasses of lemonade—it was freshly made,

not from a can—pulled out the other chair, and sat down across from me. "Sorry, I don't have any ice," she said.

I took a swallow from the glass. It was good, not too sweet. Rita watched me, but I wasn't able to meet her eyes. I looked instead at her thick fingers wrapped around the glass. The nails were neatly filed, painted a babyish pink.

"So I heard you were married," she said, "but I don't see any ring."

"I was," I said. "It didn't work out."

"Any children?"

"No."

"Me neither," she said wistfully, which surprised me, as I had not imagined for one minute that Rita wanted children. I made no response and a brief, studied silence fell between us. "So you're a famous writer now," she said.

"I wouldn't say I was famous."

"Well, you are around here."

I shrugged. "What about you?" I said. "What are you doing?"

"Oh," she said. She brushed her hair back in the familiar gesture that forced me to look at her face, that puzzling combination of Rita and not-Rita. "I'm still writing. I've almost finished the novel. It's over a thousand pages, though. I guess I'll have to cut it to get it published."

So that was it, I thought, the "business proposition." I was to help her find a publisher for a book she had been writing for twenty years.

"I work so slowly," she said. I did a quick mental calculation, less than fifty pages a year. "I've been busy with other things, of course. And my health has not been good."

"But you're nearly done," I said. "That's great."

Rita took a sip of her lemonade, allowing another heavy pause between us. "Do you think so, Maxwell?" she said. "Do you really think it would be great if I finished my novel?"

It was always games with her, I thought, and I was sick of playing already. There was a time when she could have baited me in this way for an hour or so and I would have gone along, reassuring her of my good intentions toward her, driven by lust to excessive civility, but those days were gone. What I really wanted now was to get as far away from her as I could. "What is it you want from me, Rita?" I said.

"I want to show you something."

"The novel," I said, keeping my voice interest-free.

She laughed. "No, Maxwell, not the novel. It's not finished yet." She pushed her chair back noisily and stood up, leaning on the table with the care of someone who expects to suffer in the process. I noticed a hectic flush rising from the fold of her neck to her cheeks, and a rough exhalation escaped her, not a groan but harsher than a sigh. "It's in here," she said, leading the way to the darkened, cluttered room. I followed her, consoling myself with the observation that this brought me closer to the street. Rita switched on a floor lamp which shed a dull light over a table laden with pottery. She took up a piece and held it out to me. "It's this," she said. I accepted it, as I was evidently intended to, and turned it over in my hands. It was a section of a bowl, poorly made of hard, red clay, the rim imprinted with rough scoring, such as might be made with a stick. The clay was of uneven thickness, but smooth and cool to the touch. There was something about it, a lack of artifice, a naiveté that was not without charm. "What is it?" I asked.

"It's a thousand years old," Rita said, taking it from me. She took up another piece, a flat disk, chipped at one corner, scored at the edges like the other. "Look at this one."

"Really?" I said. "How do you come by it?"

She smiled her it's a secret smile, her wouldn't you like to know smile, which always infuriated me. "I'm the agent for it," she said. "It's extremely valuable. This stuff here is worth a million dollars and there's more to be had when I go back to New Mexico."

I laid the disc on the table, careful to place it well away from the edge. So Rita, lovely Rita, hadn't just gained a lot of weight, she'd also lost her mind. Did she really think I would believe a million dollars' worth of antiquities had somehow made its way through history to a rickety table in this mildewed shack in the City that Care Forgot? Actually one could hardly find a better place to hide it—her neighbors were doubtless criminals, but they weren't likely to steal a bunch of broken crockery. I ransacked my brain for something to say, something that would release me from this suffocating room. Rita picked up another bit, a plate-like piece, and raised it toward the lamp. "This is my favorite," she said. I was struck by the alteration in her profile, which had once been very fine, though she'd always had a weak chin. Now she had no chin. Malcolm was right, her skin was sallow, unhealthy, the crescents beneath her eyes looked bruised. Time had gone hard on her, worn her down, *her*, who had been so rebellious, so uncompromising. As she set the plate back among the curious rubble, my irritation turned to sadness, and I resigned myself to accepting whatever story she had to tell. It wouldn't be true, any of it, but it would be revealing. "Where did you get this stuff, Rita?"

"From the Zuni," she said. "I was out there with them for a long time. They're a matriarchal culture, you know, they don't much trust men. I got pretty involved, trying to help them deal with the Bureau. I'm the only white woman they trust. The museums are wild to buy this stuff, but the council is afraid they'll get cheated, so I agreed to handle it for them."

"Is that where you went when you left Vermont?"

"No," she said. "Not right away." She turned to me with an absurdly coquettish smile that suggested she detected the subtext of my question—when you left *me* in Vermont, when you ran away from *me*. "Danny and I went to Alaska first. You can make a lot of money up there. We worked in a fish canning factory."

"Good Lord," I said. "I hope you finally bought a pair of practical shoes."

She laughed. "I did. I had to. It was very strange up there. It's light all the time. The factory runs in twelve-hour shifts, everyone drinks a lot of coffee. In an odd way, I liked it, but maybe it was because Danny was happy there." She waved her hand across the room. "It's all in there," she said, "in the novel."

I followed her gesture through the gloom to a table strewn with debris: piles of audio tapes, a walkman, envelopes stuffed with paper, several bags of chips—did she live on potato chips?—crumpled tissues, a stapler, a coffee cup, and in the midst of it all, with a narrow space cleared all around like a castle brooding over a moat, a stack of four white stationery boxes with a pair of reading glasses neatly folded on top. On the floor, leaning against one of the table legs, was the battered typewriter case I recognized across the expanse of twenty years. It had spent a month of its mechanical life on the kitchen table in my cramped apartment in Vermont. I'd written a brief note on it once, which came back to me in its entirety—*Back at 10. adore you. M.* "So you're still using the Olivetti," I observed.

"It's a real problem with the novel," she said. "I was in Arizona for a few years and my landlady there let me use her computer, so some of it's on a disc. But most of it is typed. Somebody told me editors don't even look at typed manuscripts anymore, they want everything in an e-mail. Is that true?"

I considered Rita's question. The old anecdote about Thomas Wolfe's manuscript arriving at Max Perkins's office in an orange crate came to mind. "They'll still look at manuscripts, but they don't like it," I said. "And it goes against you, right at the gate; it proves you're out of touch."

This amused Rita. "Out of touch!" she said. "That could be the title of my book. That's the point, isn't it?"

"Is the title still *Dark Witness*?" I said.

"You've got a good memory, Maxwell."

"I know," I said.

She wiped the back of her hand across her forehead. "It doesn't have a title right now." A thousand pages, I thought, and no title. Her forehead and upper lip were damp. It was stifling in the room and she was rubbing the palm of one hand with the thumb of the other, an odd habit which I attributed to nervousness.

"So when you left Alaska, you went to New Mexico," I said.

"Not directly. We went down to Spokane and stayed there for awhile, downtown in this old hotel, until we ran out of money. Danny went off the deep end; she really lost it in Spokane, and she wound up in the rehab center, so I was broke and they threw me out of the hotel. I didn't like Spokane. Spokane is really America. That's where they test products to see if Americans will buy them. One day I just packed up the backpack and the Olivetti and hitchhiked to Arizona. That was tough. I almost got killed doing that. Truckers should pretty much all be rounded up and shot. Except the women."

I imagined Rita, the real Rita, standing on a highway in the rain, somewhere out there, Out West, with her backpack and her typewriter case, dropping her raised thumb to her side as the eighteen-wheeler fastens her in its blinding headlights and she hears the rapid downshift of the gears. It would come to a stop

95

well past her; she'd have to run to meet it, clamber up through the steam rising from the tires into the dark interior of the cab. "Women truckers?" I said.

"Sure," Rita replied. "There are women truckers, Maxwell. It's a real subculture. They're mostly farm girls who couldn't take the abuse and got out. A woman trucker saved my life. She loaned me the deposit on a little place in Tucson. She tried to talk me into being a trucker too; they make good money and you're really on your own, but that life didn't appeal to me."

"No," I said.

"I mean, I could have done it, but it just seemed so pointless. So I found this place in Tucson, a little house on a ranch, and the landlady, Katixa Twintree, she said I could work on the ranch for part of the rent. I got a job waitressing down the road, so I was OK there for awhile. Katy is half Basque, half Indian, quite a fierce individual. She had a girlfriend, Mathilde, French, a real bitch. Katy is fantastic. I was completely in love with her, and Mathilde was completely jealous of me, so it was a mess. I couldn't sleep at all. I was writing a lot. Katy asked to read it; she was very excited by it, that's when she loaned me her computer, which made Mathilde insane. There was a huge scene. Katy just let Mathilde and me fight it out, she is so wise, and Mathilde left. So then I moved in with Katy and I guess that's the happiest I've ever been. Katixa Twintree was it for me, the love of my life."

As Rita told me this ridiculous story, my eyes wandered around the dim room, trying, without much success, to make out what was actually in some of the stacks of rubble on the various tables. At her concluding remark—which I took to be rather pointedly directed at me, as if she imagined she still had the power to wound me—my attention returned to her, and I saw that she was so moved by her own history there were tears standing in her eyes. This irked me. "So why aren't you still with her?" I asked coldly.

She gave me a wan smile. "I guess she was too good for me, Maxwell," she said. "Just like you." She brought her hand to her chest and the color drained from her face, even her lips turned greenish. She took a few steps toward the bedroom. "I have to lie down," she said.

I followed, my irritation replaced by a flutter of panic. "Are you all right?" She gained the bed, falling across it with a groan, face down. I stood in the doorway gazing at the unappealing bulk of her. Her sandals, slipping from her feet, made two sharp raps on the floor. Her skirt was pulled askew, revealing the network of broken veins inside her knees. Her ankles were bruised, swollen, and the soles of her feet were filthy. As I watched, she rolled heavily onto her side so that she was looking back at me. "Would you get me a glass of water?" she said.

I went to the kitchen, relieved to have a mission, poured out the remains of Rita's lemonade, rinsed the glass, and filled it with water. "I've got to get out of here," I said softly. There was a back door; I could easily have snuck out that way, but it was a dishonorable course. As she always had, Rita was putting me through a moral exigency. I thought of my cozy house in Vermont, and of Pamela, my neighbor, my friend and my lover, who would know exactly how to preserve her integrity and still get the hell out of Rita's kitchen. I longed for her, not to hold her close, but to be in *her* kitchen, to sit at her polished oak table while she prepared our afternoon coffee, to hear her aimless conversation as I watched the slanting sun flicker among the bright leaves of the geraniums blooming lavishly in the window. Light, Light, I thought. Not this shuttered obfuscation, not this universe of lies.

I turned off the faucet and carried the dripping glass through the sweltering gloom to Rita's bed.

She had turned onto her back and propped herself against the pillow, her skirt neatly spread over her legs. She was breathing slowly, consciously, her hand still open across her heart. She took the water without comment and drank half the glass, then motioned for me to set it on the table at the foot of the bed. This allowed me a close view of the clutter around the television, which included a plate of desiccated cottage cheese peppered with something that looked suspiciously like mouse droppings.

"Thank you," Rita said.

"Are you better now?"

"I'm not getting any better," she said.

I made no response to this self-dramatizing statement. It occurred to me that the whole thing, from the invaluable pottery to the unfinished novel to her physical frailty, was a lie. She was making it up as she went along. There was no "business prop-osition," she had just wanted to get me into her wretched life and see if she could make me feel responsible for it. Outside a cat fight flared up, a brief interlude of yowling, then it was quiet and the only sound was Rita's measured, phlegmy breathing.

My eyes settled on a stack of paperbacks next to the disturb-ing cheese plate. They were cheap romance novels, their lurid covers featuring women in distress, barely constrained bosoms, swollen lips, streaming hair. "How can you read this stuff?" I said.

Rita sniffed. "I just read it to pass the time. It's harmless. It's better than television." I picked up the book on top, anxious to avoid the vision of Rita, sprawled before me, defending her intellectual pursuits. The passionate but terrified damsel on the cover had pale eyes and a mass of golden curls, very like Rita. I wondered if this had influenced her choice. The title was something absurd.

"Will you do something for me, Maxwell?" Rita said.

I put the book down, careful not to upset the stack. "Is it the business proposition?"

"Yes," she said. "There might be something in it for you."

"I'm really fairly busy, Rita," I said.

"It wouldn't take much of your time."

"Is it to do with the pottery?"

"Yes. It is. There's a gallery uptown that deals in pre-Columbian stuff. I wrote to the guy and sent him some photos, but I don't have a phone so I had to ask him to write back, but he hasn't done it. He's probably suspicious because I don't have a phone. I'm not well enough to go clear up there; I don't have a car and the bus stop is nearly a mile, besides, if someone like you went to talk to him, well, he'd take it seriously."

"But I don't know anything about pre-Columbian art," I protested.

"You don't need to know anything. You just have to tell him you've seen the stuff in the photos and you know me and it's not a hoax or a scam. He'll be excited about it; he'll be over here like a shot trying to get it for nothing. It might be good if you were here when he comes, so he won't try to take advantage of me. I know what this stuff is worth."

"So, basically, you just want me to vouch for your character, is that it?"

"Sure," she said. "That's it."

I had not, thus far, looked Rita in the eye, but at this point, I did. She held my gaze in that icy, still, calculating way I remembered, which had once so unnerved me that I gave in, looked away, agreed to whatever she wanted. There, disguised by puffy flesh, were the same limpid windows to her mercenary heart. Did she remember how she had reduced me to shadowing her, to crouching in the snow outside a window, too mortified to move? Did the two hundred dollars, a full month's rent, that she took from the envelope in my sock drawer weigh more than a feather on her conscience? Even now, in desperate straits, alone, unloved and unlovable, she looked upon me with thinly disguised contempt. A hint of a smile lifted the corners of her mouth. What was I going to do? Let her down? Wouldn't that just be typical.

"How recklessly you've lived," I said.

"Well, Maxwell," she said, disengaging her eyes from mine. "We can't all be successful."

I sneered. "Is that your best shot?"

"I could give you maybe five percent of the deal," she said.

I laughed. "You really are incorrigible, Rita. Do you seriously imagine you have anything I want?"

She brought her hand back to her heart. The color in her face drained again, but not because she was struck by my irrefutable assertion. Her voice was confident. "You'd give your soul to have written my novel," she said.

I glanced away, to the room where the boxes gathered dust in the gloom. It occurred to me that they might be empty.

"Go ahead," Rita said. "Have a look. You know you're dying to."

I turned back, regarding Rita narrowly. Another suspicion had come to mind, that I would find myself in those pages, or Rita's version of me. Of what happened between us. She raised her head from the pillow, her lips parted in a menacing smile.

"I really don't have the time," I said, consulting my watch.

She dropped back onto the pillow. "You always were such a coward."

"Right," I said. "Let's leave it at that. Great seeing you, Rita." I headed for the door, fully expecting some further indictment of my character, some final cut, but she was silent. As I unlatched the screen and stepped into the blinding wall of heat, she moaned, turning ponderously toward the wall. I closed the screen behind me and went out to the street, scattering cats in my wake.

I had lied to Rita. I wasn't particularly busy, in fact I was at loose ends that day, as I had been for weeks. My work wasn't going well, I was avoiding the desk. As I wandered about my rented apartment, the confrontation in that depressing house began to take on color and depth, until I was convinced something had happened. I called Malcolm, who agreed to meet me for drinks near his store. I was eager to talk about Rita with someone who had known her when she was what I now thought of as the "real" Rita, the bewitching Rita, who had disappeared for twenty years and reappeared as a slovenly harridan to reproach me with the desert that was her life. Her parting remark, a continuation of an argument we'd had long ago, rankled me. Clearly, in Rita's view, my modest success only proved the justice of her charge: as a writer I was eager to please, as a man, I was afraid to live.

"Well, look where it got you," I said to the specter of Rita, hovering about me as I changed my shirt. I caught sight of my torso in the wardrobe mirror; was there a thickening at the waist? Pamela had been after me to join the local gym. "Exercise," I said. "Healthy food, hygiene, air, light, life."

"How well did you know Rita?" I asked Malcolm. We were conveying our full martini glasses to a toadstool-sized table in the bar.

"You mean when we were in college?" he said. We sat down and pulled our chairs in close. "I guess I knew her about as well as I could." His smile was wry; of course he'd slept with her.

"Did you ever read any of her writing?"

"No," he said. "We weren't that intimate. I didn't know she was interested in that sort of thing until she left to go up there . . . where you went."

"So she was secretive about it."

"She was." Malcolm speared an olive. "Was it any good?"

"It was different," I said.

"In what way?"

In what way? In a way that made us all sick with envy. Even the professor was torn between his excitement to have such a student and his despair at his own turgid prose. Rita's plot was simple enough, a love triangle, a tale of abandonment and revenge. But it wasn't the plot that took the reader by storm, it was the style. "Brutal yet elegant," the professor suggested, which was about right, about as close as I could get. Rita sat there, placid and opaque as a cat, while we heaped on the praise. "It's the speed that gets me," one of us opined, "it's like lightning." "The world is so sensual," another exclaimed. "It's lush and hot, but somehow it's invigorating." My turn came around. What did I say? "Original, intriguing." Something like that. After class Rita came up to me and asked if I'd go have a drink with her and say a bit more. "Yours is the only opinion I really value, Maxwell," she said. "Just between us, you're the only one up here who can write worth a damn, including Simon." Simon was the handsome professor; Rita was rumored to be having an affair with him. I took her arm, gratified. Later, when I cared, she would retract this statement. When it suited her, Rita would tell me that I was, in her opinion, just another talentless hack.

"So, did she ever get anything published?" Malcolm asked.

"No, I don't think so."

"Then it couldn't be too good, right?" he concluded.

"Right," I agreed.

After our third round of martinis, Malcolm called home to say he wasn't coming for dinner and we walked over to Galatoire's where I switched to whisky and ate a piece of fish. Several old acquaintances stopped by our table to tell me I hadn't changed. One, a pretty, vapid realtor who had sung in a band in college, enthusiastically informed me that she had seen one of my novels in a bookstore. Malcolm told me about his children: one was doing well, another had stolen a car from a priest. Well, borrowed, he brought it back the next morning. We left the restaurant and went to several bars. It felt good, drinking, exchanging witticisms about the scene, laughing, eventually shouting. At the end, I left Malcolm on the phone, begging his wife for a ride home, and stumbled across Esplanade to my apartment in the Faubourg. I'd forgotten about Rita, my novel, Pamela, my waistline. I burst into Donna Elvira's aria about how much she wants to tear out Don Giovanni's heart. A dog, investigating a garbage can, paused, offered himself as an audience. *Sì*, I sang. *Gli vo' cavare il cor. Sì*. The dog, evidently impressed, sat down. "That's Donna Elvira," I confided, moving on. "She's been betrayed." I turned the corner to my street. The door was, I reminded myself, the third on the right. It was dark, but I could make out the concrete steps and flimsy iron rails, what my neighbors called "the stoop," on which, in pleasant weather, they were inclined to sit and chat with the passers-by. Sociable town, I thought. It really wasn't a bad place at all. Gradually it dawned on me that there was something on my stoop. It appeared to be an enormous cloth bag, stuffed and drooping over the rail. To my horror it moved, it rose, it came at me out of the darkness. "Maxwell," Rita said. "You've been drinking."

"Exactly right," I said, veering past her. "Exactly right and now

I'm going to sleep." I pulled my keys from my pocket, but too eagerly; they slipped through my fingers and clattered to the pavement. Rita, for such a large person, was quick. She snatched them up and went ahead to the door, "Poor Maxwell," she said, "you need help." In a moment the door was open and she stood inside looking out at me.

"I need help," I agreed. I waved my arms and stamped my feet. "Help! Help!" I shouted. "A woman has broken into my house."

Rita came down quickly, shushing me. "Stop, Maxwell. You'll wake your neighbors." She tried to take my arm, but I brushed her away. "You really shouldn't drink," she said. "You never could hold it."

"Get away," I said. "Stay away from me." She had placed herself between me and the stoop. "Stop it, Maxwell," she said. "You're acting like you don't know me."

"I *don't* know you," I cried. "You're not Rita. You've killed her, somehow, out there, out West. You studied her and you know a lot about her, but you're not Rita. You're an impostor." I dodged around her, reached the steps, but somehow when I got inside she was so close behind me I couldn't shut the door. I plunged into the dark interior. Rita followed, closing the door and flicking on the light switch. "I need a drink," I said.

She leaned against the bookcase, watching me, breathing heavily, her lips parted and her tongue protruding. Panting, I thought. Like a dog. I availed myself of the whisky bottle on the sideboard, and poured out a glass. How was I going to get rid of her now that she was inside, blocking all the space between me and the door? "Why are you here, Rita?" I said, keeping my voice calm.

"I felt so bad after you left today," she said. "I didn't mean what I said. I was angry at you because you didn't want to help me."

Her voice was shaky, edgy. If she started crying I would never get rid of her.

"OK," I said. "Apology accepted."

"I didn't think you would come, and I wasn't ready for how it made me feel to see you again, so I said stupid things. And you were so cold, Maxwell. You never used to be so cold."

"I've changed," I said.

"And now you tell me you think I'm an impostor, that somehow I've killed myself . . ."

"I didn't mean it. I'm drunk. And I'm tired. I want to sleep."

"I need to sit down," she said. She advanced to the couch and collapsed among the cushions. It was an uncomfortable product of the folded-futon school with a decidedly backward pitch, which she accommodated by leaning forward and planting her feet wide apart. Her big skirt billowed over her ankles so that only the pink toenails peeked out. She patted her hair down absently. "Could I have a glass of water, Maxwell?"

I sipped my whisky, contemplating my options. Should I drink more in the hopes of becoming comatose, or try to sober up and devise a plan to get her out of my living room? I was drunk enough to be stupid, I was sure of that. Rita was looking around the room, appraising the furnishings. "It's nice in here," she said. "It's cool, too." Her eyes came back to me, settling upon me with a proprietary complacency that sent a warning chill through my circuitry. "You've really done well for yourself, Maxwell. I knew you would."

I poured water from the seltzer bottle into a glass and handed it to her. "No ice," I said. "Sorry." Rita took the glass and drank half of it. "Seltzer," she said. "I haven't had that in a long time. Do you have any vodka to put in it?"

"No vodka," I said. "Only whisky."

Rita held out the glass. "That would be fine," she said. "Whisky and soda is a good drink."

I poured a thimbleful into her glass, keeping my eye on my own hand, which seemed detached from me, a long way out there. "Just a little more, if you don't mind," Rita said. I poured in enough to turn the water golden. Rita took the glass and sipped at it, making a sucking sound that was loud in the stillness of the room.

"The thing is," she said, "what I told you wasn't true. I felt bad about that. I wanted you to know the truth."

"Why does it matter?" I said.

"I think it matters," she said. "I think of myself as an honest person. The truth is, Katixa wasn't the love of my life. I thought she might be for awhile. I was pretty worn out after Danny, and Katy was strong and quiet, and she was excited about the novel. Danny never read any of it; she wasn't much into reading."

"Danny was into barroom brawls, as I recall," I said.

"That's true." Rita laughed. "Danny liked to fight. Katy was the opposite; she was always calm. But after a while I realized she didn't really know anything about books. She was excited about my novel because she'd never really read one before. To her I was a genius. I couldn't talk to her about it, about where I was going with it, what I was doing. Writing is such lonely work, well, you know."

"I do," I said, pouring myself more whisky. The comatose option was looking attractive.

"At that point I thought maybe my problem was that I couldn't be happy with a woman. So I got disenchanted with Katy and pretty soon I was bored with the ranch and every animal and every person on it, except Bolo, the Mexican, a real Indio. One day he had had enough of it too, because Katy was suspicious of us and making his life hell, so he said, let's get out of here and I went with him."

"So that was it," I observed.

"Was what?"

"Your problem. You couldn't be happy with a woman." I was standing behind her and she turned to look at me, clutching her glass, her eyes flashing in the old way with the pleasure she took in telling a tale. She gulped her drink and plunged on.

"I still don't know; maybe it was. Bolo and I stayed together for awhile, drifting around, until we just drifted apart and I wound up on the reservation. While I was there I thought about my life a lot and I realized there had only ever been one person who loved me in the way I wanted to be loved, and that was because he was smart enough to value the best thing about me, which is my writing, because he knew, among other writers, among my peers, I was good, I was doing good work."

"And that person would be me," I said.

"Sure, Maxwell. That's what I realized. You were the love of my life, but I didn't know it then. I was too young. I didn't have any experience. I didn't know enough to know it."

"You knew enough to steal my rent money."

"Are you still mad about that?" she said testily. "Is that why you're so cold to me?"

"I'm not mad about it. But I'm curious to know, since you're such an honest person, how you justify stealing from the person you now recognize as the love of your life."

"There's nothing intrinsically dishonest about stealing money, Maxwell. Money doesn't have anything to do with integrity; that much is clear. Just read a newspaper. You knew I took it, and you knew why."

I appeared to myself as I was that day, impossibly naive,

rushing into the frigid apartment, calling her name, but only once, because it was instantly clear that everything was altered; her typewriter, her shelf of paperback books, her furry slippers, were gone. It was an hour or two later when, in an agony of suspicion, I opened the empty envelope in my sock drawer. Of course, I thought. Of course. "You took it because you didn't give a damn about me," I said. "And you're right, I did know that."

She sipped her drink, arranging her skirt in an absent, coquettish way that infuriated me. "I was desperate," she said.

A chill arising from that night, when I'd understood how thoroughly and willfully she had betrayed me, rose up between us and it had a fierce, sobering effect. "Aren't you always desperate, Rita?" I said. "Aren't you desperate right now? Isn't that why you're here? To see if you can use me somehow, because you're so desperate?"

"I don't understand," she said, gasping for air. She leaned forward over her knees so far I thought she might fall on her face. "I'm not well," she said breathlessly.

I watched her, pitiless as a god. She was a pathetic woman who meant nothing to me. "I'm calling a taxi for you," I said, taking up the phone. As I spoke to the dispatcher, Rita sat up again and commenced mopping her brow with a handkerchief she extracted from her sleeve. When I hung up, I lit into her again. "What you don't understand," I said, "is that there's nothing noble or brave about the way you've lived. You didn't finish your novel because you didn't know how to finish it. No one kept you from finishing it, because no one cared whether you finished it or not. You made everyone who might care suffer because you knew you would never finish it." I'd wounded her. The sweat pouring from her brow mingled with tears. A series of racking sobs convulsed her. "It doesn't take twenty years to write a novel," I continued. "It might take five or seven, but not twenty."

"It's almost finished," she pleaded.

"I'm almost finished," I said. "But not quite. You're a liar and not a very careful one, Rita, you always have been. You lie about things that don't matter. Do you think anyone believes you've got a million dollars' worth of art objects in that shack you live in, that you have the confidence of some Indian tribe, that you're here selflessly laboring on their behalf?"

Rita was hardly listening to me; she was too absorbed in her own suffering. Her handkerchief was a sodden ball she dabbed at her flushed face; her mouth was ajar. The sight of her, perspiring on my couch, enraged me. "Get up, Rita," I said. "Get up and get out of here." I wrestled my wallet from my pocket and peeled off a fifty-dollar bill. Rita struggled to her feet, gripping the sofa arm with both hands, and made a tottering progress toward the door. I was ahead of her, throwing it open.

"It's not fair," she said, through her tears. Her hand came up fast when she saw the money I held out to her, my arm stretched fully to escape actual contact with her flesh. She took the bill and looked out at the street, which was humid, hot, and dark, then back at me. "I've read all your books, Maxwell," she said. "I'm a much better writer than you'll ever be."

Something happened then; it was the worst thing that happened. She was looking past me at the couch and I had the sensation she might push her way back to it. As I stepped forward to block her, she must have turned toward me, because I bumped into her and knocked her off balance. I saw a flash mixed of confusion and consternation cross her features, and then she was falling forward, over the steps. Not many steps, but she fell for what seemed a long time, without a sound save the dull thud of her body against the concrete. She lay still, face down on the sidewalk, the mass of her flowered skirt rising over her like a tent.

There was a moment, before I could move, when I considered closing the door and going to bed. But of course I did no such thing. I leapt down to the pavement and bent over her, whispering her name. A hand came out from somewhere and grasped my ankle. Another unworthy impulse, to kick free of her, passed, as she turned onto her side and looked up at me dazedly. "Are you hurt?" I said.

"I don't know," she replied.

I offered my hand, which she gripped with surprising strength, pulling herself to a sitting position. I was as close as I had been to her, close enough to recoil from the rank smell of unwashed flesh and fetid breath coming off of her. "You slipped," I said.

Groaning from somewhere deep within, she pitched forward to her hands and knees and billowed up beside me. To my relief the taxi turned at the corner, pulled up at the curb. Rita stood panting beside me, still clutching the bill I'd given her. "You pushed me," she said. The cab driver got out and opened the door for her.

"This lady has had a fall," I told him, ushering Rita inside. She didn't resist. "Are you sure you're not hurt?" I said, but Rita wasn't looking at me. She was folding up the bill I'd given her and sticking it into her sleeve. It occurred to me that the driver might not be able to change a fifty, that some further unpleasant scene might occur, so I handed him a twenty and told him to keep the change. This caught Rita's attention. "That's too much," she said.

"For God's sake, Rita," I said. "It's my money."

"It's too much," she repeated.

The driver frowned at her. "I'll give her the change," he said. "I'm not trying to rob nobody."

"She's very upset because of the fall," I said, slipping him another bill, both of us careful to keep our hands beneath the window. "She lives on St. Ann, close to the old cannery."

"Sure," he said. "Don't worry, I'll take over now." I looked in at Rita. The cab was air-conditioned, the light was on. She was arranging her skirts, brightening up. There was a skinned patch on her temple, bruising rapidly, and the palms of her hands were scratched; that was all I could make out. A taxi ride was something of a novelty to her, and she was now concentrated on controlling every aspect of it. "Goodnight, Rita," I said. She looked up, fixing me with cold eyes. "You pushed me," she said. I backed away and the cabbie slid into his seat. Giving me a jaunty salute, he pulled the door closed and carried Rita away, into the night.

The next morning I battled my way through the precincts of an impressive hangover to the computer screen, where I spent an hour tracking down a ticket to Vermont. I called Malcolm, who expressed no surprise at my decision. "Too hot for you," he said. "You'll be back in January." Next I called Pamela, who detected something urgent in my tone, something amiss. "You sound upset," she said. "Is everything OK?"

"I'm just drinking too much. I'm not getting any work done. It's too hot and I miss you."

"I miss you too," she said. "It's lovely here. My tomatoes are ripening. There was a moose in the road this morning, heading for the hardware store."

My spirits lifted. "Tomatoes. A moose," I said. "Sounds like paradise." Pamela agreed to meet me at the airport. I packed my suitcase, called the landlord and then the taxi. The driver was not the one who had rescued me from Rita; I made sure of that by calling a different company.

Two weeks later, the boxes arrived. The postal slip had the New Orleans zip code, so I thought I'd left something behind and the landlord had sent it on. But when the postman pushed the sizeable package across the counter, I saw that the return address was Malcolm's. "It's heavy," the postman warned me. He was right.

Malcolm had put the flimsy stationery boxes in a sturdier carton, previously used to transport a case of wine. He'd shoved a little newspaper around the sides and laid a folded sheet of paper with my name printed on it across the top. I knew what was in the boxes the moment I lifted the flaps, but a firm impulse of denial allowed me to read Malcolm's note with more curiosity than apprehension. I admired the unexpected legibility of his cursive hand. He'd had a Jesuit education. *Dear Max*, he wrote. *I'm sorry to tell you that Rita Richard has passed away. The circumstances were grisly. She called me just after you left, asking for your address in Vermont. When they found her, my phone number was in her purse, which is how I got involved. We had to get rid of everything in her house. These boxes, addressed to you, were among her things.*

When you get this, give me a call and I'll tell you all about it. Hope you are well. Your friend, Malcolm.

Rita had scrawled my name and address on the lid of the top box, obviously intending to package them at some later date. Her handwriting was scratchy; the pen she'd used was running out of ink. I could see her, bearing down on the name of my town, on the zip code, determined that I should not get off easily, that I owed her something yet.

I lifted the boxes and put them on the floor next to my desk. A sensation of dread, such as Epimetheus must have felt when his bride told him who had manufactured her luggage, stole upon me and I recalled that in some versions of that story it is he, and not the lovely, curious, deceitful Pandora, who opens the box, thereby unleashing all the evils of this world. I felt, as I had not in her living presence, perilously vulnerable to Rita. Purposefully I strode away from the boxes to the kitchen, where I paced back and forth. After a thorough examination of the contents of the refrigerator, I picked up the phone and called Malcolm.

No one knew exactly when or how Rita had died; her neighbors had nosed her out. By the time Malcolm arrived, the police were zipping her into a body bag; they were wearing gauze masks and had brought in blowers to air out the rooms. They had found her, face up, on the floor in the second room, between the pottery shards and her novel. Malcolm explained that he was little more than an acquaintance, which provoked the detective. Why would she have your phone number in her purse, he wanted to know, and when Malcolm said she had called looking for a friend's address, he repeated the question. The landlord arrived, visibly flustered. Rita had failed to pay the rent for two months and he had sent her an eviction notice. The police came through, dragging Rita in the bag like an unwieldy carpet. The landlord turned white, rushed out to the porch and vomited into the azalea bush. This made the detective suspicious. How well did the landlord know Rita, he wanted to know. In fact he'd never even seen her, he insisted. He'd inherited the house at his mother's death a year previous; Rita was already in it. Usually she paid her rent on time. The landlord was shaky, so they all went into the kitchen for a glass of water. There they discovered the garbage, alive with maggots. The landlord had to go outside and sit on the back steps, his head between his knees. "I don't see why you're so upset, if you didn't know this lady," the detective observed.

"It's my house," the landlord protested. "There's a corpse rotting here, who knows how long, the place is crawling with maggots. Of course I'm upset."

LIMERICK
COUNTY LIBRARY

"You're mighty sensitive for a landlord," the detective said.

After some conversation it was discovered that Malcolm and the landlord had both gone to Jesuit, two years apart. Malcolm had played football with the landlord's brother. "Dickie Vega," Malcolm said. "You remember him. This guy is his older brother, Jack Vega."

The detective took their names and addresses and told them he would be in touch. The police were sealing off the house until the results of the autopsy came in. Malcolm and Jack Vega agreed to walk over to Matuzza's and have a beer.

The autopsy report said Rita had died of natural causes; therefore, the detective told Malcolm, he was closing the case. He had determined that Rita had no living relatives, so the city would undertake the disposal of her remains. He had also learned that Rita had a criminal record: she'd stolen a truck in Nevada.

"What kind of truck?" I asked Malcolm.

"Big. A semi. They found it in Texas."

Jack Vega had a dumpster dropped off at the house and he and Malcolm went through Rita's possessions. "Just junk," Malcolm said. "There was a checkbook with about twenty dollars in it and a fifty-dollar bill on the table by the bed; that was it. No insurance policy, no personal mail, just bills, clothes, a bunch of broken pottery, some books and those boxes I sent you. I had to do the garbage; Jack couldn't go in there."

"So you threw all the pots out," I said.

"It was junk. It was all broken."

"She thought it was valuable," I said.

"Right," Malcolm said.

When I got off the phone I sat at the kitchen table drumming my fingers. So that was it, the end of Rita. A bloated corpse rotting on the floor of a dilapidated shack. Total worth: seventy dollars and some broken pots. How long did she lie there, in the sweltering heat with the slatted light creeping in across her body, later withdrawing, leaving her in the dark, with the skittery night creatures, the roaches, the mice, her unfinished novel? I called Malcolm again. "Did they estimate when she died?" I asked.

"Yes. It was the day after she called me, looking for you."

"And when was that?"

"It was after you left."

"So, a few days later."

"No. I guess it had to be the next day. She knew you were gone, though. She said she'd seen you the night before and you'd forgotten to give her the address. I figured she made that up."

"No," I said. "I didn't see her. I was out with you that night."

"I knew that. I knew she was lying. She lied all the time, but it didn't do her any good."

"No," I agreed.

"So, what's in the boxes? Love letters?"

"I don't know. I haven't opened them yet."

"I thought about throwing them out with the rest of the junk, but Jack said we should respect the wishes of the dead. That doesn't mean you can't throw them out. Maybe you should. Maybe you don't want to know what's in them."

But I knew what was in them. In my study I stood with my toe pressed against the boxes. I pushed against them, but they didn't budge. "You pushed me," I heard Rita say.

I was painfully conscious that I had lied to Malcolm. I wasn't afraid of being caught in the lie; no one was interested in Rita's last night on earth. The coroner's verdict, natural causes, meant no mysteriously ruptured organs, no suspicious bruises or contusions, and Rita was ill, anyone could see that; she'd said as much herself. I discounted the possibility that the fall Rita had taken at my apartment had contributed to her demise. What bothered me about the lie I'd told Malcolm was that I couldn't take it back without appearing suspicious. I was stuck with it.

Just as I was stuck with the boxes. I backed away, to my chair, where I sat regarding them steadily, as if I expected them to move. I considered my options, assessed the ebb and flow of curiosity. Once I opened them, I thought, Rita would be back in my life with a vengeance. Did I have a moral obligation to allow this to happen? They contained, I could not doubt it, her life's work, all she had to show for herself, and she had directed them to me as the person most likely to vindicate that life, which had ended in ignominy. She was right to choose me; I was situated to be of use. I could send the manuscript to my agent, or directly to my editor, and it would receive a fair reading. Neither of them would be delighted to receive a thousand loose pages typed on various machines with no backup, by an author who was unknown and dead, but they would look at it and if it was as good as Rita said it was, consider the risk.

And what if Rita's novel was a success. It wasn't unprecedented. Virgil, Emily Dickinson, Franz Kafka, Fernando Pessoa, John Kennedy Toole, to name a few, had left the business arrangements to their friends and relatives. Pessoa's chest contained thousands of loose pages. Kafka had outdone everyone by extracting a promise from his friend Max Brod to burn everything at his death, burn *The Castle*, burn *The Trial*, but Brod, to the relief of posterity, had broken that promise. I'd visited Kafka's grave in Prague and laid the requisite pebble on the slab to hold the wispy Czech in place, and another on the loyal Brod's tablet nearby. What kind of friend made such a request? Kafka was dying for years. He had plenty of time to burn whatever he wanted burned. Didn't he possess a stove, a box of Czech matches?

If Rita's book was published, my part in that process would be a feature of the packaging. Like Brod, my celebrity might rest upon it. I would be the generous writer of little note who went to bat for a work of genius by an artist who had died precipitately, crushed by the indifference of a heartless industry. The public eats that stuff up: the fantasy that artists—unlike, say, businessmen—are driven by warm fellow-feeling. In their devotion to the religion of art, they are ever seeking, without self-interest or crude competitiveness, to celebrate genius, wherever it can be found. There wouldn't be any money in it for me. To maintain my status as a selfless benefactor, I'd have to give all the proceeds to a worthy cause—the Zuni might be a good choice, whoever they were, or some lesbian/gay alliance. I might get some interviews out of it. Who was this fascinating author? How did the manuscript come into my possession? I'd be free to reinvent Rita anyway I chose: a courageous adventuress, a seductress, a poète maudite, a helpless victim of her own integrity and her impossibly high standards, a self-serving user, a tramp, a liar, a thief. Rita would belong entirely to me.

This scenario amused me, though it was doubtless far-fetched. The fact that, twenty years earlier, everyone in a small writing program in Vermont had agreed that Rita was gifted didn't mean she had parlayed that gift into a masterpiece that would take the publishing world by storm. It was more likely that the novel was a disjointed, flawed narrative, an overblown self-absorbed chronicle of Rita's battle with the world. There might be flashes of brilliance, but no discipline.

One way to find out. All I had to do was open a box.

How close to finished was it? Was there, in its pages, some exaggerated version of myself, of those few months, so long ago, when Rita and I gave up on sleep in favor of drinking and sex?

Would I find myself dissected, a squirming, quivering creature, flayed and pinned open on a page, my panicked heart throbbing for all to see?

I got up and took a closer look at the boxes. In the top corner of each one was a number, one through four, an effort at order. She had, I knew, written my address sometime between her departure in the taxi that night and her death, a period of not more than forty-eight hours. There might be a note to me with a more precise description of her wishes, perhaps an apology for having insulted me and some mollifying language designed to make me feel guilty if I failed to comply. Wouldn't that be just like Rita?

I slipped my fingers under the edge of the box and eased the lid up with the care and trepidation of an expert trained in munitions disarmament.

Twenty years ago, for a poor graduate student on a stipend of four thousand dollars a year, two hundred dollars was a lot of money. I bought my clothes at secondhand stores, attended college functions for the free food, otherwise subsisted on vegetables, and drank draft beer with my peers at the local pool hall for a dollar a pitcher. My father was long dead, and my mother, who lived on a small pension from the US postal system, didn't approve of my decision to leave Louisiana in search of an unlikely career. Even if she'd had the money, I was too proud to ask her for help. Within a few days everyone knew Rita had left not only me, but the town, and I was the subject of pitying looks and kind remarks, which galled me. I certainly wasn't going to augment my image as the local cuckold by revealing that Rita had robbed me as well. As I straddled Rita's novel, the recollection of that humiliation assailed me, stayed my fingers, straightened my spine. I stood there, drinking it in, a bracing bitter potion from the past. How had I made up the loss?

I'd gone to the real estate office and arranged to pay twenty-five dollars for that month and an extra twenty-five on the regular rent for the next seven months. I searched the local paper for part-time work, but there wasn't much. Because I was teaching and taking classes, my hours were limited, the town's economy was depressed, and I didn't have a car. Eventually I found a minimum-wage weekend job selling tickets at the movie theater in the mall out on the highway. There was a bus that let me off in the parking lot. It wasn't bad. I got all the popcorn I could eat and I could see the movies for free. I cleared about twenty dollars a week, which made a big difference in my lifestyle. I bought a good pair of duck boots, and, because I could pay for the pitchers more often, my entrance at the pub was greeted with hearty enthusiasm. I wrote a story about a guy who works at a movie theater. He becomes obsessed by a beautiful young woman who comes in alone every Saturday night, buys two tickets, and sits through two films, the seven and nine features, whatever they are. He starts to make up a life for her, a reason why she has to be away from home and off the street from seven to eleven every Saturday. It can't be because she loves the movies; most of them are idiotic. He starts following her after the shows. He knows where she lives, where she buys her groceries, what café she meets a girlfriend in, where she buys her clothes. Finally she has him arrested for stalking. He loses his job. It turns out she's a freelance movie critic. It was called "The Flicks," and it was the first story I placed in a reputable quarterly, the *Oliphant Review*. I was paid ten dollars, plus copies.

I never told anyone Rita had robbed me. It was one of those secrets I kept because it was pleasurable to keep it; I have a few. Years later, in a novel, I had a male character steal money from a lover in a similar fashion. My character pauses in the midst of the heist and considers taking only half the money—he knows how poor his lover is—but I doubted that Rita had given me that much consideration. It was a failure on my part to imagine a character as heartless as Rita.

The phone rang; it was Pamela. Did I want coffee? I wanted to get away from those boxes, but I didn't tell Pam that, perhaps didn't know it myself until I was safe in her kitchen. The windows were open, there was a vase of bright zinnias on the ledge, the light was lambent, the air fragrant and cool. Pamela in her man's shirt spattered with paint, her hair mussed, her eyes unfocused from the hours of close work at her easel, leaned over me with the coffee pot and pressed her lips against my neck. "Have you been working?" she asked.

"Yes," I lied. After the coffee, I lured her into her bedroom, where we passed a few amiable hours. Then we were hungry and decided to go out for sushi. We were pleased with ourselves for wasting the afternoon on sex. We ate a lot of raw fish and drank several bottles of sake. After that we walked around the town, looking in the shop windows, greeting neighbors out with their dogs, and stopped at the bar for a nightcap. It was midnight when I left Pamela at her kitchen door and crossed the lawn to my own. In the course of the evening I'd forgotten about Rita's novel. But when I turned on the light in my study, there it was, a reproachful cardboard cairn near the trashcan. I considered the possibility that sake and whisky were incompatible substances, that, in some sense, this explained the difference between East and West. If mixed in a glass, would they separate? I put this question in the same to-be-explored category as the contents of Rita's boxes. My desk didn't send out even a beckoning vibration as I wandered past it on my way to my bed.

In my dream Rita was young again, but I was as I am now. It

was a snowy scene and she was teasing me to race her to a fence post across a field. She didn't have a chance, I told her, she was wearing open-toed shoes with high heels and I had on sturdy boots. But she insisted. She was lovely, her eyes bright, cheeks flushed. Her hair, stuffed under a fur hat, broke out over her forehead in golden ringlets. "Come on, Maxwell," she said. "If you're so sure of yourself, what have you got to lose?" At length I agreed. She took off ahead of me, surprisingly quick in those impossible shoes, and I followed. My feet were heavy. I ran in dream slo-mo, while Rita dashed ahead. As I hobbled along I came across one of her shoes, then the other, abandoned in the snow. When I looked up she was sitting on the fence, laughing. I clutched her shoes to my chest. It was snowing hard; I could barely see, but I could hear her, laughing, and calling out to me, "I win, Maxwell. I win."

The telephone was blaring. I fought my way free of Rita's taunting and snatched the receiver, pressing it to my ear, distracted by a sudden sharp pain in my groin. "Maxwell," Rita said. "Did you get my novel?" In the process of throwing the phone away from me, I lost my balance and slid off the edge of the bed to the floor. When I opened my eyes, I was flat on my back, looking up at the red point of the phone charging light, which only went on when the receiver was firmly lodged in its cradle. I looked down at my erection, fading fast after having been squashed when I rolled over on it to answer the call. "Rita," I said. "God damn you."

In the morning my mood was blacker than my coffee. Rita was stomping around in my head like a devil with a pitchfork, and not Rita-lite, but Rita as she was on the last night of her life, with her harsh breath, her forearms like hams, her petulance, her frank, flamboyant destitution, Rita who had suffered and lived and stolen large machinery, Rita the accuser, the avenger.

I could hear the boxes chortling on the floor.

I was twenty-five that year. Rita was just twenty-one, but she was way ahead of me, erotically speaking. My experience had been that some women liked sex, others endured it, and others were looking to make some kind of deal. Rita was avid, rapacious, it was sport to her, yet I never doubted for a second that she was in deadly earnest, in it to prove to herself that she was the gold medalist. Now it strikes me that she was suicidal, trying to get some man to kill her, but I didn't have a clue about the dark side of anything then. I was an innocent, and Rita knew it.

So did Danny Grunwald, the scary little dyke Rita left me for, who reigned in an unofficial way over a pool table at Cues, the bar we frequented, daring "suckers" to play a game with her, swilling cheap bourbon and probably shooting something besides pool. Now and then she picked fights with tough men twice her size, went out in the alley and came back bloody, pleased with herself. She liked to tease Rita about me. "Hey, gorgeous, what are you doing with that loser?" "What has he got that I don't have, honey? I'm sure it ain't that big." That sort of thing. I thought Rita's laughter was embarrassment, that she was as appalled as I was.

That night we'd been drinking for hours. Rita was tense and, before I knew it, furious at me for joking with a fellow student at the table next to ours. The fight went on back at my apartment, all night and into the next morning, when I took a shower and went to the college to teach my class. I knew Rita had a class in the afternoon, so I didn't expect to see her until evening, by which time we would both have been sober for more than twelve hours and in a condition to patch up our quarrel over a plate of vegetables and a pot of strong coffee. But the hours slid by and Rita didn't appear. I read all twenty of my students' writing exercises—describe a situation in which you regretted your behavior. There were always a few who had no regrets; invariably these were boys. Why were girls so full of regret? One, a clever one, regretted taking my class.

At length I was hungry. I chopped and steamed the vegetables, made the coffee, ate at the table while reading a Chekhov story for my Modern Masters class. Finally it was ten p.m. and no Rita. I put on my boots, coat, hat, scarf, gloves, and went out into the icy world in search of her. I figured she would be at Cues; if not, I could drink with friends.

She had been there, but she was gone, no one knew where. Things I failed to notice: sympathetic looks on the faces of my friends, absence of Danny Grunwald. Hours later I slogged back to the apartment, certain she would be there—she had an early class in the morning—but she wasn't. I fell asleep on the couch. When I woke, the sun was up and Rita was passing through the room on her way to the shower.

"Where were you?" I inquired from the cushions.

"Wouldn't you like to know," said Rita.

I got up and we argued a little more over breakfast, but we were both too tired to keep it up. She made up some lies, she'd been at the library, time slipped away, she'd met up with friends, gone out until it was too late and she was too drunk to walk home. We went to the college together, parted amiably enough, agreed to meet at the diner for dinner; it was payday. I waited there for an hour before I ate a grilled cheese and went out to find her. It was snowing. I tried the library, which was bloody unlikely, and then Cues. As I came into the block, I spotted Rita leaving the bar, walking briskly away from me. She looked so purposeful I didn't call out to her. I wanted to know where she was going. I scurried along, close to the wall in true detective style. She turned into an alley halfway down the block. Stealthily I followed. It was a narrow street of one-room cottages with half-closed porches, lined up one against the other. They had been built for factory workers long ago, when there was a factory. Now they were run-down, derelict, but occupied. The residents stowed their wood on the porches and the smoke from the stovepipes hung over the narrow passageway, coating the walls, the trashcans, the banked snow, the passers-by, with grime. Rita stamped her feet at the entrance to one of these, stepped up to the porch, opened the door without knocking, and went inside.

I stood in the snow for several moments, unable to make up my mind to move. I had a fair idea of what I would find if I followed Rita, if I knocked on that door, and I wasn't up to it. I made my way back to Cues and joined a table of aspiring writers, most of whom would eventually find employment in the tech industry. I drank half a pitcher of beer, glowering at the pool table where a cordial game was underway, absent the belligerent heckling of Danny Grunwald. One among us pointed out that our professor's new novel had gotten a lackluster review in the daily *Times*. It was generally agreed that his books were boring.

I was thinking about the stovepipes on the shabby houses in the alley. My apartment, which I'd rented in blissful August ignorance, had a fireplace that warmed an area of about four cubic feet in front of it. I knew now, too late, that a woodstove was the indispensable appliance in this climate; one could sooner go without a refrigerator. Whenever Rita and I visited friends who had a stove, we stayed late. At home we sat at our typewriters wrapped in blankets; at night we took our clothes off after we were under the covers in bed. In the morning, against the advice of the authorities, we warmed the kitchen by leaving the oven door open. If I had a woodstove, I concluded, Rita might be with me now.

Maybe that was it. Maybe Rita had just gone to the little house to warm up. I finished my beer. Energized by this crackbrained theory, I bid farewell to my friends and stumbled out into the snow, around the corner to the smoking cottage. I wanted to tell Rita that we would move right away, as soon as I could find a place with a woodstove.

The porch was piled with carefully stacked, evenly split wood, a professional job. The axe hanging from a nail on the wall had an edge that gleamed. I didn't doubt that Danny could swing it. The wood filled the space, only an area in front of the door was clear. This door, obligingly, had a curtainless window in it. Heedless as a fish biting down on a lure, I stepped up to it and looked inside.

It was a scene out of Bosch, complete with demons, and, belching from the cast-iron stove that squatted in one corner, the flames of hell. The furnishings were meager, a card table, two metal folding chairs, a sagging sofa the color of dried blood, and a side table with a red shaded lamp that partially obscured my view of the main event. This was going forward on a bare mattress in front of the stove. Rita was naked, on her hands and knees, back arched, hair wild, features contorted in the ecstasy that so often resembles pain. Behind her, equally naked, Danny Grunwald was gleefully occupied, ramming something cylindrical into Rita's delicate parts. She laughed and talked as she worked. Mercifully, I couldn't make out what she was saying, but I could imagine it, which may have been worse, though I doubt it. Her eyes, which had always struck me as piggish, glittered like burning coals, and her tongue flicked sprays of saliva into the air. She was built in square blocks with large, sagging breasts attached at the front.

Her skin, in that diabolical light, looked like meat. They were both turned away from me, so I was free to look as long as I wanted. What exactly was that instrument Danny was using on Rita? Which orifice was she penetrating with it? I pressed my face against the glass. Rita dropped her head forward and made a bucking movement with her hips. Danny leaned over her back and grasped one of her breasts.

The voyeur, spying on lesbians, who is detected and invited to join in the fun, is a stock feature of pornography. Men would pay to watch a man in my position; I knew that, but the last place I wanted to be was on the other side of that door. I don't deny that the sight of Rita disporting herself excited in me feelings hitherto unknown. It was hot, all right, but the heat, which became every moment more unendurable, wasn't in my cock, it was in my brain.

I stepped back, clutching my head. Wiring was shorting out in there; I could hear it, sputtering and popping. I had to sit on the step because my knees were rubbery. A pile of snow, dislodged from the eaves by my collapse, dropped down on my neck. Great, I thought, and then, who cares? I didn't bother to brush it away. I was busy experiencing, for the first time, the bracing shock of total betrayal; there really is nothing so cleansing. Born alone, die alone, love a mirage, life a cruel joke, death standing in the wings, the one who really wants you, the only one who cares. I was in pain, but I didn't feel like crying. I had the sense that something hidden had been revealed, not about Rita, who was clearly, from here on out, the "other" the "not me," but about myself. My expectations had been banal. I was stupid.

Eventually I got up and walked back to my apartment. I tried to read Chekhov, who had a lot to tell me about betrayal, but I couldn't concentrate. I turned out the light and sat in the dark, fell asleep on the couch again. Sometime before dawn Rita came in. I didn't ask her where she'd been, which provoked her to trot out a veritable circus of lies. "Rita," I said, "I was on the porch tonight, watching you through the window."

This was a hammer blow and she staggered beneath it. Come on, I thought, tell me I didn't see what I saw. After a moment she said, "Danny thought someone was out there."

"Well, Danny was right."

Then we had tears, apologies, protestations, vows, it went on for a long time. She wanted me to go to bed with her, which I told her was impossible; I was fresh out of anything hard enough to satisfy her. More tears, buckets of tears, suicide threats. When she was exhausted we got into bed and fell asleep with our clothes on. Towards morning I woke up, found her straddling me, thought, what the hell, and did it. We got up, wary as cats, ate breakfast, minimal, polite conversation, and I went off to my class. At the door Rita kissed my cheek and said in her most earnest manner, "Maxwell, you have to forgive me."

I didn't forgive her, but I thought of her during the day and that part of me that had hardened toward her thawed around the edges. Simon, the handsome professor, stopped me in the hall to say he was hosting a dinner party for a visiting writer, just a few faculty, selected students. "We thought of you and Rita." This cheered me up. Real food, I thought, probably meat, wine from regular-sized bottles. "That would be great," I said. "I'll tell Rita."

The snow stopped, the sun came out. I had a few student conferences, all about their regrets or the lack of them. In the afternoon I walked across the campus, pondering Rita. What *was* she? Did she know herself? When I got to the apartment, I flung my bag on the couch and called her name. Just once. That's when I noticed the Olivetti was gone.

*

I took my coffee into my study and stood at the desk, looking down at Rita's boxes. In some bizarre, chimerical fashion, she was in them, impatient for me to make up my mind and get to her. "Come on, Maxwell. You know you're dying to." Not just yet, I thought. I grabbed my notebook and went out to the screen porch. It was a strategy. When it was sunny out, and the desk did not entice me, sometimes it worked. I laid out my arsenal, pen, notebook, coffee, and sat looking out at my yard. Birds were chirping, the air was warm and damp, my geraniums, the only flower I can grow successfully, sparkled in the early morning light. Pamela's deep-purple clematis, cared for on her side of the fence, billowed over and made a lush display on mine. My eyes rested upon an oblong flagstone half hidden by a spirea bush, the grave of Joey, my late companion, dead, by my reckoning, three years now, felled in his youth by a cancerous growth resulting from injections the vet said he needed to keep him alive. He was a big cat, fourteen pounds, powerful, but shy and goofy, not much of a hunter; his prey slipped through his paws. Sometimes when he tried to jump up on a chair or when he was tearing up the stairs, he missed his mark and landed on his side or his butt, always with an expression of discombobulation that made me laugh. His last months were hard. The tumor grew so large it pushed up into his neck, making it difficult for him to turn his head. Still, the vet said, he wasn't in pain, he was eating, cleaning himself. Occasionally he tried to catch a bug or stalked a squirrel. He tired easily, but didn't sleep much. In the afternoons, he searched me out and leaned against my leg until I took him up and held him in my arms. Then he would sleep for a few minutes, always waking with a start, as if he'd been dreaming and waked into an unfamiliar world.

His death was sudden and awful. The tumor, evidently full of fluid, collapsed, sending a blood clot to his brain, or so the vet speculated when it was too late. For perhaps fifteen minutes he screamed in agony, crashing against the walls, tearing at the air; I couldn't get near him. Then he was still, but breathing hard, the air rasping in his throat, his eyes wide, swarming with terror. By the time I got him to the vet he was gone.

I was angry about it all, angry at the vet, angry at myself, angry at death. I brought Joey home, got out my shovel and dug his grave. I wanted it big and deep, and I dug for a long time until I was standing in a hole above my knees. At the start I wept, but as I worked I began to take an interest in doing a good job. One could do worse than be a grave-digger, I thought. I wrapped his body in an old pillowcase, laid it in the hole, down in the earth where nothing could disturb him. Then I shoved all the dirt back in on top of him. Pamela gave me the stone; she had it left over from a path she'd made in her own garden. Later she planted the spirea, which required no maintenance.

Down in the earth. The phrase arrested me. I took up my pen to write it down, feeling it might be the start of something. To my chagrin, the pen was dry. "For God's sake," I said. I pitched the pen in the trash as I passed through the kitchen on my way to the desk. The boxes were waiting, quoting Rita. "Among other writers, I was good. I was doing good work." It struck me anew as an uncharacteristically modest remark for Rita to have made, but she was in her conciliatory mode, trying to convince me that I should care what happened to her, now that no one else did. I chewed the end of my pen. It was sad, Rita's life, especially the end, dragged off in a sack by the police, her corrupted body disposed of at the public expense. Did they bury her somewhere, in some pauper's field, or was she incinerated along with other undesirables, the vagrants no one claimed, shoved promiscuously into a furnace, like the doomed dogs and cats at the pound? And then what? Did they scrape the ashes into plastic bags and cart them off to the landfill?

Whatever they'd done, that corporeal substance, once beautiful, later unlovely, containing the turbulence that was Rita, was no more. For twenty years she'd been a dim figure from my personal past, and there had been moments, not many, when I wondered what had become of her. Now I knew. She had entered the historical past, that densely populated terminus for which we all hold a ticket. She wasn't going to call, she wouldn't turn up at my door, she couldn't know what I did with the heap of cardboard and paper she had directed to me in an effort to entangle me further in her miserable fate. What, after all, did I owe her?

Pursuing this question, I went back to the porch. I was thinking of Franz Kafka and Max Brod. I'd heard somewhere that when Kafka read his dark stories to the very small group of his admirers in Prague, he was so convulsed by laughter he could hardly get through a sentence. It occurred to me that Brod had disregarded Kafka's wish that his work be consigned to ashes, not because he couldn't bear to deprive the world of the complete works of his friend, but because Kafka was just that, his friend, someone with whom he had shared pleasant hours of camaraderie, conversations, laughter, someone he missed. Publishing the manuscripts was a way to extend the friendship he had enjoyed, to keep his brilliant, quirky, ironic friend alive.

Though we had briefly been lovers, there was no sense in which Rita and I were friends. She had seldom been even routinely kind to me. I didn't miss her. If offered the opportunity to call back to life Rita or Joey, I knew I would choose, without hesitation, the cat.

Sound thinking, salubrious, this was the way to go at it, out in the warm, clear light of day, without sentimentality or superstition. I sat down to the notebook, calling up the phrase that had tantalized me earlier: *down in the earth*.

I'd been mistaken. It wasn't the beginning of something new; it was the end of this story. I looked out over my property; I'd want a spot as far from Joey as possible. There was a mass of invincible pachysandra thriving in the sandy soil near the fence. I could pull it aside and lay it back on top when I was done. It would grow in by fall.

I was calm; I wasn't vengeful. I'd give Rita a chance. I would put the boxes in a hard plastic case—I had a number of them I used to store my own manuscripts—space-age stuff that would withstand a century or two of the old diurnal roll. I swallowed the last of my cold coffee. Then, with a sense of purpose and well-being, I went out to the shed to get my shovel.

THE OPEN DOOR

At breakfast Isabel said, "You hate men because you want to be one."

"Oh please," Edith replied, buttering her toast so hard it broke. The only sliced bread the baker had was the equivalent of zwieback, unless you wanted salted pizza dough. "Spare me the deep psychology."

Isabel shrugged. "I don't mind," she said. "I like men too."

Edith poured hot milk into her coffee, thinking how pleasant it would be to throttle Isabel. "You're just lucky I'm not one," she said.

Isabel turned her attention to the newspaper, folding and flattening it next to her plate. As she read, she stroked her thick forelock back against her temple, a gesture that sometimes filled Edith with desire, but this morning it was just one more irritating thing about Isabel. This trip was a mistake. Edith should absolutely have refused the invitation, but there was nothing to be done about it now. She must just get through it somehow.

Last night's reading had been a fiasco. The audience was made up of women who had come to flirt with one another and couldn't be bothered listening to the poet they had paid to hear. When she looked up from her text, Edith saw Isabel whispering into the ear of a voluptuous blonde dressed in red elastic and stiletto heels. At the reception Edith was trapped by a tweedy Italian academic who confessed herself to be a passionate lover of Emily Deek-in-son. "Wild-a nights, Wild-a nights," she intoned, closing her eyes tight and holding her glass of prosecco out before her like a microphone. Edith looked past her to see Isabel and the blonde clutching one another's forearms to keep from collapsing in laughter. Afterwards, in the taxi, Isabel opened the window, which she knew Edith hated. "It's so warm," she said, rosy and flushed from the wine and the attention, leaning her head back against the seat; she was practically purring. Edith looked out the other window and saw the Colosseum whirl into view like a murderer leaping from the shadows. Isabel saw it too, and regarded the monstrous rubble dreamily. "How I love Rome," she said. "Couldn't we live here someday?"

Not on your life, Edith thought as she watched Isabel brush her toast crumbs off the newspaper onto the carpet.

"I see the government is dissolving again," Isabel observed without looking up.

Twice in two days Isabel had accused Edith of hating men. Did this mean she was thinking of leaving Edith for a man? An Italian, no doubt, one of these swaggering babies who Isabel would claim understood her because they were both Latins. While Edith had to spend the morning at the university talking with students who had read her poems in bad translations, Isabel was lounging in some piazza with this man, chattering about how wonderful Rome was and how impossible it was to live in a college town in god-forsaken Connecticut, what a word, and of course the man would try to say Connecticut, fail miserably, and they would both laugh until they wept.

Edith answered another question about Emily Deek-in-son.

Yes, she was an early influence. All American poets had to address that astonishing gift sooner or later; and then a young woman raised her hand and asked a very specific question about a translation of one of Edith's poems, which this student thought was inaccurate. It was the word "choke" in a poem titled "Artichoke," which the Italian translator had rendered *cuore*, "heart." Edith found this an entirely interesting and appropriate question. She explained that the word "choke" meant the tough matted center of the vegetable, an inedible part, not the heart, which was soft and delicious. The English word had a verb form as well, "to choke," which meant "to strangle." Edith grasped her neck between her hands, pretending to choke herself.

"*Strozzare*," the student said. "We have a pasta called '*strozza-prete*.'" The audience laughed while Edith waited for the translation. "Priest-strangler," the student said. Edith beamed at her. "Exactly," she said. "You could say, 'priest-choker'."

At the reception, Edith kept an eye out for this young linguist, and when she made her shy approach, sipping nervously at her cup of Coca-Cola, Edith motioned to her, cutting short a conversation with one of the organizers of the event, who was explaining how important it was to promote the free exchange of culture. "Your question was interesting," Edith said. "What is your name?"

"Amelia," the girl said. She was thin and awkward, her dark hair cropped short and her myopic eyes made large by the thick lenses of her glasses. "I am an admirer of your poems for many years now."

"I wish you were a translator," Edith said. "You have obviously given more thought to the difficulties than some professionals."

"It is difficult," Amelia agreed. "Especially poetry like yours, which is so passionate."

Edith patted the young woman's bony shoulder. "Thank you," she said. "Thank you for saying that, Amelia."

It was what Isabel had said, years ago, when she finally read a manuscript of Edith's poems. Well, it was almost what she said. "It's surprising," she said. "I think of you as cold, but these poems are passionate."

Edith had mulled over this qualified praise for some time. To Isabel a person who did not act upon every impulse was cold, and it didn't occur to her that the systematic repression of powerful emotions resulted in a hard surface that contained a core of molten lava. She had no interest in the Victorians, whom she dismissed as prudes. Edith's reticence was a source of amusement to her. She liked to parade around the house in scanty gowns; after her bath she sat naked on the chair in the bedroom, rubbing scented oils lovingly into every inch of her flesh, her expression as serene and rapt as a child in its mother's arms.

She was affectionate in an overpowering, leonine way, grabbing Edith by the waist or arm or even by the neck, and hauling her in for unexpected hugs and kisses, and if she detected any flinch or tremor of reluctance, she would push her captive away, saying, "Oh, you are so cold. What will it take to warm you up?"

Better she should ask, Edith thought, what it took to make me so cold. She knew all about Isabel's happy childhood, the darling of her Italo-Spanish parents who traveled widely, always moving in bohemian circles, the mother a painter, the father a successful photo-journalist. But when Isabel politely asked about her childhood, Edith knew she had no real interest in the subject, so she only said, "It was a farm in the midwest, completely boring." She didn't describe the poverty, both spiritual and physical, the bone-aching work which was her lot from the time she could lift a plate, the battle zone of the shabby domestic scene, the parents whose hatred for one another found expression in rage at their children for being born, the strong possibility that when she was grabbed by the arm, the waist, the neck, what she was about to receive was not an expression of affection. "I didn't come to life at all until I went to college," Edith said, and left it at that, sparing Isabel the details of those painful years as well: the paralyzing social awkwardness, the repulsive sexual encounters with young men whose sole desire was to insert their penises into a woman's, any woman's, mouth, the yearning after beauty, the discovery of poetry, of a world so utterly exotic and exciting that she had to take it in slowly, like a starving child, who longs to gorge but can barely manage a spoon of gruel. She entered the classroom too awed to speak and sat quietly in the back, her heart racing as the professor elucidated what was to her the syntax of flight. She still remembered the night, alone in her dorm room, when she read an Elizabeth Bishop poem and collapsed across her bed in tears of such agony and joy that she could hardly get her breath. This was life! This was hope, even for her!

And then she fell in love with Madeleine, the brainy editor of the student literary magazine, and then it became possible to be a feminist, to stand with other women against the oppressive maleness that made history one long description of the battle for territory, and then she began to write poems of her own, and the black ink flowed like the black nights of her childhood, replete with nightmares, terror, and blinding flashes of light. The poems were edgy, shocking, they took on the world she hated and reduced it to rubble. The first professor she showed them to called her into his office and sat looking at her incredulously for a moment before he said, "I can't believe you wrote these, Edith. You seem so mild-mannered."

Edith smiled at this recollection as she stood at the mirror combing her hair back and gathering it into the twist she had taken to wearing because Isabel said it made her look like a French aristocrat. Poetry made manners possible. It was her vengeance; she needed no other. She applied a gloss to her lips and darkened her eyebrows, which had gone nearly white in the last year. She felt a quiver of anxiety about the evening ahead. She had skipped a talk at the conference so that she and Isabel could have dinner alone together in a place where no one knew a thing about them.

At the restaurant Isabel enthused about the pleasures of Rome, how beautiful, exciting, and charming it was, how lively the populace, how stunning the women and fashionable the men, how she felt she had come home at last, and Connecticut was some other planet where she had been taken hostage and forced to pursue her art among aliens.

"Is there much of a dance scene here?" Edith asked, pouring out another glass of the excellent wine the waiter had recommended.

Isabel pursed her lips. Of course it wasn't New York, but yes, there was. She had spent the afternoon at a studio run by an old school friend, and she could report that everything was highly professional. The company had just come back from a successful tour of Japan.

Italian dancers in Japan, Edith thought. That would be worth seeing.

"The Romans know how to live," Isabel continued, "sensibly and well. Yet it's remarkably inexpensive. Our apartment, for example; nothing remotely comparable could be found in New York, Paris, or London for the price."

This was true, Edith admitted. All the Americans who had accepted the lodgings arranged by the conference were jealous. They were stuck in an ugly modern building in an uglier suburb, an hour from the university by a crowded and unreliable bus. Isabel had taken one look at the address on the conference brochure, pronounced it impossible and got on the phone to her various Italian connections, some of whom, Edith knew, were former lovers. The apartment belonged to the sister of a man Isabel had seduced when she was in school, many years ago, as she pointed out, and now safely married to a Milanese. He visited Rome only a few weeks a year, there was no possibility that she would even see him. They had the place for a month, staying on two weeks after the conference ended. It was in a six-story art deco building near the Vatican, complete with marble floors, tall windows, and surprisingly modern plumbing. It even had a sunny study which opened onto the courtyard, where Edith sat with her espresso each morning drawing pictures of flowers in the margin of her blank page.

"The apartment is great," Edith agreed. "Though I couldn't live with the street racket for more than a month."

Isabel rolled her eyes up to show her impatience, then spoke to the waiter who had arrived with a platter of fried vegetables. He was a cherubic young man, all curls and chubbiness, with an expression of solicitous serenity that Edith envied. He listened to Isabel's chatter, nodding agreement while his eyes wandered over the table, checking the levels of the wine and water bottles, then settling on Edith's face. He knew she was an American, that she didn't speak Italian. At the start of the meal, he had enjoyed a brief exchange with Isabel in which she had told him they were from New York. It was easier, Isabel explained when he had gone; no Roman had heard of Connecticut. Now, as Edith allowed herself to be examined by the mild-eyed young man, Isabel asked, "Do you want grilled fish?"

"No," she said. "I want pasta."

"La pasta," the waiter exclaimed, evidently pleased. He ran down the list of offerings, most of which Edith understood: with peas, with shrimp, with salmon, with tomatoes and garlic, with porcini mushrooms.

"*Funghi porcini*," Edith said, and Isabel too looked gratified. When the waiter had left them, Isabel reached out and patted her hand. "Isn't this a great restaurant? I haven't been here in twelve years, but nothing has changed."

"It's very nice," Edith agreed. She knew this was an inadequate response, but she felt oppressed by Isabel's hard-sell campaign to make her agree that everything in Rome was superior to everything in America. It was an interesting place to visit, certainly, but there was much that Edith found horrific: the packs of thieving children who would take the shirt off one's back if they could get it, the kiosks displaying walls of the vilest pornography, the embarrassing television shows where even the news announcers wore low-cut tops with push-up bras and seemed intent on seducing their audience, the ceaseless roar of the traffic, the young men on motor scooters cruising through even the narrowest streets, so that one had to be prepared to press against the wall at every moment, the ubiquitous cellphones, often two or three at a restaurant table, with the diners all shouting into them, the monuments to tyranny and superstition every twenty feet or so.

And then there was the strain of watching Isabel, who was practicing denial with the terrified concentration of a fiddler in a burning building. She was glancing appreciatively around the room; it was cave-like, but bright, because the walls were white.

There were racks of wine bottles cleverly stored in various alcoves. "It's lovely," Isabel said, soaking in the agreeable atmosphere. "And the food is excellent. I could eat here every night."

But you can't, Edith thought. And when you can't, what happens then?

Isabel and Edith had lived together for ten years, sometimes harmoniously, but sometimes not. They met at a party given by one of Edith's colleagues at the college where they were employed, a painter who flattered herself that her wide range of acquaintance made her parties newsworthy events, though in fact she only invited people from the college who were connected to the arts and had some small professional standing as well as endless opinions with which they had long ago succeeded in boring one another past rage. Edith had just won a prize for her second collection of poems, *Sullen Vixens*, and she was being congratulated by a Victorian scholar whose insincerity was a marvel to see, as Edith knew he had tried mightily to block her tenure. As she accepted his fake enthusiasm, she saw Isabel smiling up at her from a wicker couch in the sun room. Isabel in the sun room! She was wearing something diaphanous, a dark blood-red, billowy in the skirt but fitted in tight folds across the bodice, leaving her shoulders and neck exposed. She had one arm stretched across the back of the couch, and she was leaning forward to fish a few nuts from the bowl on the coffee table. There were a lot of big plants ranged around the room and several of the painter's brightly colored canvases on the walls, so Isabel appeared to be sitting in a tropical jungle. She had her dark hair pulled back tightly, her lipstick was blood-red, like her dress. Edith thought of a Frida Kahlo self-portrait: it was as if Frida had taken a look at herself and been actually delighted by what she saw.

Later Edith asked her hostess who the woman in red was. The painter raised her eyebrows as high as she could get them and pressed her lips together in a bizarre grimace which she evidently thought proved she knew Edith well and understood the erotic significance of her question. "Wouldn't you like to know," she announced joyfully. "Well, I will tell you. She is the new instructor in the dance department, Isabel Perez. She's from Costa Rica originally I think, or maybe Paraguay. I can't remember. Come along and I'll introduce you."

And so they met. The painter introduced Edith as "our wonderful poet who has just won a very important prize. We are so proud of her." Edith, made miserable by the idiotic falsity of this introduction, could only nod and stretch out her hand, which Isabel took gingerly saying, unfortunately, she knew nothing about poetry. There was just a trace of an accent, not much more than the odd incorrect stress. Edith could think of no response to this observation, so she smiled and nodded her head, hating the painter from the bottom of her heart. As soon as she could, she slipped away to the drinks table and poured out a full glass of bourbon.

When she looked back into the other room she saw that Isabel had gotten up from the couch and was talking animatedly to a tall black man in a white suit, Mabu Adu of the French department. She could tell by the way Isabel was working her mouth that they were speaking in French.

Edith shivered. She had not hoped to meet anyone even mildly interesting at this party; she had certainly not expected to fall in love. She found it difficult to stop looking at Isabel. Michael Mellon, her fellow poet, a nonentity from nowhere, rushed up to her and confessed that he had been thrilled by the news of her prize because it was so rare these days for work one actually admired to receive any recognition at all. He felt positively vindicated. "In fact," he said, "Ellen told me to calm down. She said I was acting as if I'd won the prize myself!"

Edith accepted her colleague's praise at face value. The poor man had been instrumental in bringing her to the college, taught her book in his classes, and, as she knew from various sources, had made an impassioned speech at her tenure review meeting, calling her one of the best poets of her generation. She did not doubt that he was the only person in the department who had not actually writhed in pain at the news of her selection. "What a generous man you are, Michael," she said. "Your friendship is as good as a prize to me." He blushed, and glanced about to see who was witnessing this acknowledgement of his worth. Edith followed his look and saw Isabel very near, her head tilted to listen to some pleasantry from Mabu, her eyes resting on Edith, the slyest of smiles lifting the corners of her mouth. I wonder what she looks like having an orgasm? Edith shocked herself by thinking. She returned her attention sharply to her well-wisher, who was asking her a question about a promising student whose honors thesis he was directing. They talked a few minutes more, then, when Michael spotted his wife arriving— she had dropped the children off at the soccer clinic—he excused himself and hurried away. Edith took a swallow of her bourbon and watched in amazement as Isabel disengaged herself from Mabu and made straight for her side. When she got there she said in a silky voice just above a whisper, "What thought were you having about me, just now?"

Had Edith heard correctly? Isabel's perfume, spicy and warm, wrapped around her like a sensual embrace, and Edith held her glass still only with an effort. "I was thinking," she said, "that I would like to take you to lunch."

Isabel frowned. "But where? Everything in this town is so dull."

"We could drive to the city."

"Yes," Isabel agreed. "I know some wonderful places there."

Much later, in very different circumstances, it occurred to Edith that this brief and magical exchange only proved how absurdly easy Isabel was.

Edith stood glowering at the books on the English bookshop table. How was it possible? Two collections by her arch-enemies Lulu and Mark Zinnia, one by her former girlfriend Lydia, whose poetry was always described as lyrical, though Lydia actually had the sensitivity to language of a baseball bat, and one by Malva Plume, a mawkish sentimentalist who "celebrated the body." There was also a small stack of *The Monk's Alarm Clock*, the surrealist J.P. Green's newest, which Edith had read and liked. That was it for contemporary American poetry. On the fiction table nearby, Edith spotted the Marilyn Monroe book and the new one in which Mussolini visits New York. She picked up Lulu's book and opened it to the picture on the back flap, taken, of course, by Mark. Lulu was sitting on what looked like a swing; there was a heavy chain next to her face. Her slightly protruding eyes were focused entirely on the camera. Beneath it was a list of the prizes she had won. Edith opened to a poem at random and scanned a few lines. Lulu was anxious about Mark's bad cold. Edith laughed and snapped the book closed.

The Zinnias were a golden couple, astonishingly successful given the meagerness of their talents and the tedium of their lives. They never stopped congratulating themselves. Whenever they took a little trip, like this one, there was a whole spate of poems about the trip. They wrote poems about their spoiled, mean children as if they were visiting deities. Edith recalled the last time she'd seen the vicious daughter, a dumpy, overweight child who sat down on the ottoman next to Edith, balancing a plate of brownies and a plastic glass of punch, and asked with an insinuating smirk, "Are you and Isabel going to get married?"

Before the rift, the Zinnias had been friendly to Edith, inviting her to their crowded parties where the wine was cheap and the flower arrangements were large and composed of weeds. Edith politely attended their readings, keeping her mind firmly on something else, a novel she had read, or a mental image of Isabel's naked back. What she knew about their personal lives she learned from their poems.

Edith placed Lulu's book back on the stack next to her husband's. She really had not thought when she wrote "Tame Poems" that Lulu would recognize herself as the subject. "Tame poems, docile, bleating Iambs, / no threats, no surprises." Edith thought it was harmless enough, and general as well, though there was one line near the end that clearly referred to Lulu's poem "You Protect Me."

But as soon as the poem was published in an obscure journal, everyone at the college seemed to know about it. Michael Mellon took her aside after a department meeting and told her Lulu was devastated. There were no more party invitations. Mark cut her at the graduation; Lulu was too sick to attend.

Publishing "Tame Poems" proved that Edith was angry and rash. Michael told her Mark announced at a dinner party that Edith was eaten up with jealousy, because he and Lulu were devoted to each other, whereas Isabel was flagrantly unfaithful to her. The Zinnias were powerful in poetry circles; they edited anthologies and sat on prize committees. That year Mark edited a big anthology. Edith was conspicuously absent from this collection.

Isabel laughed at the whole business. "Wonderful," she said.

"There were never any chairs at those awful parties and the food is always fish paste on white bread."

One summer night, shortly after the anthology snub, Isabel and Edith sat on their front porch splitting a bottle of champagne to celebrate Isabel's return from a course of master classes in the city. Isabel was in high spirits. "Let's walk," she said, pulling Edith up by both arms. "Let's stroll past the Zinnias' and see if they're having a party." It seemed an amusing idea and Edith slipped her arm through Isabel's thinking that Mark and Lulu had never known one moment as joyful as this one, strolling out into the quiet tree-lined street, giddy from the champagne, the warm night air, and each other's company. What if there was a party, and the guests standing on the porch looked out to see Edith and Isabel, indifferent to their feast, nocturnal and svelte, like panthers slinking past a gathering of stupid, yelping hyenas? Who would envy whom?

But when they got to the house there was only one dim light on near the back. "What is it, ten o'clock?" Isabel said, "and the Zinnias are snug in their beds." This was funny too. Edith pictured Lulu and Mark in matching flannel pajamas, plaid, or with pictures of teddy bears on them, curled up under the covers in their narrow four-poster. Long ago Lulu had insisted that Edith and Isabel take themselves on a tour of the house, and Isabel had snorted at their rickety antique bed with its thin pillows and grandmotherly quilt. "The scene of a grand passion," Isabel said, even going so far as to sit on the edge, pronouncing it "rock hard, completely unforgiving."

"Wake up, Mark and Lulu," Isabel sang out as they stood looking up at the dark house. "Your house is not on fire." Edith chuckled, then said, "Hush. They might wake up." Isabel drew her closer to the house, while she laughed and made a mock struggle. "No, no, be careful, be quiet," she said, stumbling over a yard hose. "We don't want to wake the great American poets." When they were past the porch, Isabel said, "I have such a great idea," and she pulled Edith behind a bush so that they were hidden from the street and right up against the wall of the house. "What is it?" Edith said. "What are we doing here?" Then Isabel put her arms around Edith's waist and held her close, kissing her neck and shoulder. "My Edith," she said. "You are so adorable when you are tipsy."

"Me?" Edith protested. "You drank much more than I did."

"But I am never drunk," Isabel said, kissing her on the mouth. Edith closed her eyes and gave in to the embrace. It was true, she thought, Isabel was never drunk.

Edith's blouse was unbuttoned and Isabel's halter top was around her waist when the light went on and Mark stepped out onto the porch. "What's going on out here?" he said in the tough voice of the outraged homeowner, protecting his domain. Did Mark have a gun? Edith thought. Isabel took her hand and whispered, "Run!" They burst past the bushes, clutching their clothes to their breasts and running hard until they got to their own porch. Then they staggered inside and fell on the couch, laughing like bad children.

Wild-a nights, Edith thought. The book store clerk approached and asked if he could be of any assistance.

"I'm looking for a book of poetry," Edith said. "*Unnatural Disasters*, by Edith Sharpe."

"We don't have that," the boy said indifferently. He had a long face, pockmarked skin, and a prissy British accent. "We don't carry much American poetry." He walked away to another customer who was going through a stack of travel books.

Edith went out into the street, still so absorbed in her thoughts about the Zinnias that she nearly collided with a *motorino* parked on the thin strip of cobblestone that passed for a sidewalk. When the awful business with Isabel's student, Melanie, blew up, Mark was as hateful and stupid as the rest of them. But one afternoon, Lulu had come into Edith's office, closing the door behind her and leaning against it. "I just want to tell you," she said, "that I don't think these charges against Isabel are entirely fair."

"Of course they aren't," Edith said. "But no one really cares about that much, do they?"

"Melanie Pringle was my student last year."

"Did she make a pass at you?"

Lulu's eyes widened at this thought. "No. But she's no innocent." Then, clearly horrified by what she had just said, she pulled the door open and slipped out into the hall.

"Turn it off, turn it off," Edith said, rising from her chair in desperation. "I can't look at any more breasts."

Isabel scowled. "You are so puritanical," she observed. She changed the channel to a panel show in which three women were perched on a narrow couch gibbering into one another's cleavage. Edith stalked toward the kitchen. "It's not puritanical to detest seeing women degraded to nothing but mammary glands on stilts, which appears to be the highest goal of the female in this ridiculous country."

Isabel studied the television screen. "You're jealous because they are so beautiful and they enjoy being beautiful."

"Oh, for Christ's sake," Edith said to the stove. "I am not jealous of women who choose to be bimbos." She pulled the coffee pot from the rack and poured water into the base. "Do you want coffee?" she shouted.

Isabel clicked off the television. "Yes," she called back.

Edith struggled with the espresso packet, attempting to open it with a dull knife. "There are scissors in the drawer," Isabel advised her from the doorway. Edith looked at her, scowling as the knife pulled free of the packet and the coffee exploded across the counter. "Surely you can see these women are just cows in need of milking?" she said, reaching for the sponge.

Isabel smiled. "They do love their breasts," she said. "And why shouldn't they? They're lovely. I've never wanted large breasts myself; that's impossible for a dancer. It just doesn't work to have anything bouncing around. But if I had breasts as pretty as Giovanna Bottini's, I certainly wouldn't wear mannish suits like the news announcers in America."

"Who is Giovanna Bottini?"

"The one with the talk show."

Edith tightened the top of the *caffettiera* as hard as she could, set it on the burner, and lit the flame with the sparker. So Giovanna Bottini was not the woman at the reading. "How can you have a talk show if everyone is preoccupied with presenting their breasts, and no one listens," she said gloomily. "It's depressing. It's like the poetry reading. Why have a poetry reading if no one is going to listen? Why not just have a party and spend the money on food?"

"Oh yes," Isabel replied. "It's so much better to sit in an icy little room reading to dreary overweight women in parkas who tell you how liberating it is for them to think about how much you despise men."

"I don't despise men, Isabel, as you well know. I have many friends who are men. I hate the patriarchy and with good cause, as a purely cursory reading of history will prove."

The coffee pot began to hiss. "I'll heat the milk," Isabel said.

When they had carried their cups to the table, Isabel pursued the subject. "Why do these Italian women bother you so much?" she asked seriously. "You don't mind it when I wear almost nothing and leap about on the stage. Why isn't that depressing?"

"It's completely different," Edith said. "You're an artist. It's not your body you put on display, it's your art. You've made your body into something sublime with which you express an ideal of beauty that has nothing to do with tits on parade."

Isabel considered this for a moment. "No, that's not true," she concluded. "For me, dance is entirely sensual and erotic. I don't care about ethereal ideals of beauty. I use my body as a medium for the expression of extreme states of desire."

Right, Edith thought. She set her cup down carefully on the saucer. "How can you say that to me?" she said, glaring at her own hand. She was never able to look at Isabel when she was angry.

Isabel allowed the harshness of this question to darken the air between them. "What are you talking about?" she asked.

Edith kept her eyes lowered, running through the menu of cutting replies that appeared behind her eyes. Isabel answered her own question. "You're talking about Melanie Pringle," she said. "All this is about Melanie Pringle, isn't it? All this hostility toward sexuality and beauty. I thought if we came here we could get away from all that and have a pleasant time together, but I see you've packed Melanie up and brought her along."

"Just don't tell me about your extreme states of desire," Edith said, "and maybe I won't be reminded of what they cost us."

"There was nothing extreme about it," Isabel protested. "She waited in the dressing room until the others were gone and she put her arms around me and kissed me."

"What made her think she could do that?" Edith asked coldly. "She must have been pretty confident about what your response would be."

"She's a beautiful, rich young woman," Isabel replied. "No one tells her no. She's made out of confidence, that's all she is. And when she realized I didn't care for her, she got angry and decided to destroy me."

"Was that the reason?" Edith sniffed. "That's reassuring."

"It's a stupid mess, she's a stupid girl, but it has nothing to do with us. We can't let her drive us apart; now that would be folly."

Edith felt something in her chest contracting, as if her heart had turned into a fist. "I guess it just doesn't occur to you that I might feel humiliated," she said. "That having my colleagues all fall silent when I enter a room because they've been talking about you, because they feel sorry for me, that having Lulu Zinnia, for God's sake, look at me with pity because I live with you, that I find that humiliating, and that this stupid mess, as you call it, has everything to do with us. It will probably be the end of us, especially if you lose your job."

"You care what Lulu Zinnia thinks more than what I think!" Isabel exclaimed. "How can you possibly care what a tedious bourgeois housewife like Lulu Zinnia thinks of you? You despise Lulu, you've insulted her publicly. You despise most of your colleagues, and rightfully so, they're a pack of hypocrites. What does it matter what they think of us? They already have so many horrible thoughts about us just because we're together, what will a cunning new twist add? Do you want to be like them, Edith? Tell me now, because I need to know. Do you want us to bind ourselves to their narrow, empty morality so that you can hold up your head and not feel humiliated by people you despise?"

"I don't despise Lulu, I despise her poetry," Edith corrected.

"All the more reason to dismiss her cheap sympathy."

Edith drank her coffee, though she didn't taste it. "It's not that I care what they think. I'm afraid of what they can do. You know what's in the works; you know what's going to happen when we get back. If you get sacked for harassing a student you won't be able to find a job anywhere."

"I'm not going back," Isabel said abruptly. Edith shrugged and blew out her breath. "I'm not," Isabel insisted. "I'm not going to go on trial and be judged by those lifeless puppets. And anyway, I can't go back now. I've accepted a position here, starting in the fall."

Edith was so astounded she clutched her head between her hands. "What have you done?" she whispered.

This is what Isabel had done. While Edith had been absorbed in the conference activities, Isabel had been talking, talking, talking, and making plans for them both. Her college friend had offered her a position at his academy, which operated partly for students, but was also the studio of a professional company. "I won't be teaching overweight girls who lurch around like frightened sheep," she said. "These are real dancers." She had also made inquiries at the university where Edith's appearances had been wildly popular. A new program in Feminist Studies was being planned for the advanced English students and Isabel's informants assured her that if Edith showed an inclination to accept one, a position would be offered.

"It's not that simple," Edith said. "I've been at the college for fifteen years. I have tenure, a good retirement plan. I can't just throw all that over for a job that may have no future."

"You're in a job that has no future now!" Isabel exclaimed. "If you stay there you'll end up like the rest of them, with their policies and their committees and their horror of sex and joy and life. You'll dry up like a prune. Think how happy we could be here. We'll find an apartment with a *terrazzo*. No snow, no disgusting galoshes and parkas! You'll be like a flower opening in the sun."

"There's more to life than good weather and coffee," Edith said drily. "And I don't want to be a flower."

"You're being impossible," Isabel said, getting up from the table. She went to the window where she stood looking out into the noisy street. Overhead they heard the screech of furniture being dragged across the floor; they had heard the same sound every evening of their stay, though they never heard anything dragged back. Edith sat at the table, hunched forward, her hands folded before her, and she thought, I'm sitting like an old woman. She straightened her spine and looked at Isabel.

It all felt dismally familiar. They were at the middle point of an argument they had been through a thousand times: reason versus passion, vitality versus stability. Sometimes, when Isabel was so frustrated and stymied by her career that she became depressed and Edith had to buck her up, they had even switched sides. But this time a resolution of these irreconcilable differences would have to be found, for it was not just philosophies that were at odds, but material possibilities.

Edith observed the sad tilt of Isabel's still firm chin, the downcast eyes, the line of her elegant nose casting a shadow like a blade across her cheek. She was forty-one years old, and she was panicked. Edith herself was a threat to her, being part and parcel of the intolerable status quo. Now she'll tell me America is killing her, Edith thought.

Isabel came from the window and rested her hands on the table, leaning into them. "I can't live in that place," she said. "It's like being slowly asphyxiated. I feel alive here. Rome is so full of disorder and messiness, all the things Americans are terrified of because they prefer death to life. That's why they are so in love with machines, which are dead, and why they prefer communicating with one another using code names so that they can't be identified."

Even as she was annoyed by this argument, which she had heard before, the sideline about technology amused Edith; it was so like Isabel to deploy her grievances in squadrons.

"If you care for me at all you won't ask me to go back there," Isabel concluded.

"Wait," Edith said. "I wasn't aware that I had any choice in the matter. Would you go back if I asked you?"

Isabel looked into her eyes with such desperation that it hurt Edith to see it. "I don't know," she said.

Edith pictured Isabel sitting at the end of a long table as a group of men somberly considered the charges against her. It crossed her mind that Melanie Pringle was not entirely an accident, that Isabel had, in some unconscious way, been looking for Melanie. "I don't think you should go back," Edith said. "I think you've done the right thing."

"Then you'll stay with me here?"

"I hate it here, Isabel."

"I've lived ten years in a place I hate for you," Isabel retorted.

"That's just not true. You've been trying to leave the college since the day you got there. You didn't stay for me, you stayed because the only other position you were offered was in Arizona."

"I would have gone to Arizona if it hadn't been for you," Isabel said. "That's how much I hate it there."

"I just don't think I can work here," Edith said. "I haven't written a word since we've been here."

"That's all you really care about," Isabel whined. "Your bitter, hateful poems." Then she burst into tears.

Edith was unmoved by Isabel's tears. Her head was aching and she was nauseated. "So the poetry has to go too," she said. "What do you think will be left of me?"

"I didn't say you shouldn't write it," Isabel whimpered. "I said you shouldn't care about it so much."

Edith thought her head would burst at this remark. "Suppose I tell you to stop caring about dance," she said.

"I didn't say you should give it up!" Isabel protested, drying her eyes on her sleeve.

"There's nothing you won't say when you're not getting what you want," Edith said. She pushed her chair back and staggered away from the table.

"Where are you going?" Isabel asked coldly.

"To get some aspirin," Edith said. "My head is killing me."

Your bitter, hateful poems, Edith thought. She was sitting at a table in the small whitewashed anteroom of the lecture hall, attaching strips of sticky paper to the pages of her books. There were four books, plus a loose manuscript of uncollected work. She was putting off looking at the date of her most recent poem.

She had more and more difficulty writing, and she knew it was not entirely the fault of European travel. Perhaps, she told herself, she was going through a transition, and some exciting, original work lay ahead. She need only be patient and alert, waiting to hear the new voice, to recognize the new path. Poems that came less easily would be more telling.

Or perhaps the truth was that she had exhausted the vein of her poetry and there was nothing left to draw from it, neither blood nor gold. There had been a time when her head was always filled with phrases and lines, presenting themselves wantonly for her inspection like contestants in a beauty pageant, and she went to her desk with a strange, nearly erotic excitement. Were these poems hateful? It was true that the metaphors reviewers used to describe them often included sharp edges: knives, razor blades, a surgeon's scalpel. Here, in fact, was a sonnet titled "Incision," which was ostensibly about their cat Jasper's neutering, though there was some play with the word "incisive," and the wounding, emasculating power of language. She would read that one; it would remind Isabel of Jasper, whom she missed.

They had argued late into the night. For the first time in ten years they had gone to sleep in anger, though Edith thought she remembered Isabel's hand seeking her own, perhaps in sleep. In the morning they hardly spoke, both puffy-eyed and bleary over their coffee. It was the last day of the conference and Edith had a full schedule. Isabel planned to lunch with a friend, then arrive at the university in time for the reception before the reading. As she was packing up her books, Edith said, "You don't have to come, you know. You've heard it all before."

"Don't be ridiculous," Isabel said. "Of course I'm coming."

Edith turned a few pages, scanning titles, looking over the compact display each poem made on the page. The window next to her table was open, and the warm air was damp, musty, with a torpid movement that was more like an exhalation than a breeze. August must be an inferno, Edith thought, and smiled as the legend—*The Divine Comedy*—passed across her brain. Outside someone shouted a greeting to someone else, and there was a burst of laughter. The students were affectionate with one another and almost absurdly respectful of their professors. One of the coordinators had told Edith that all exams were oral; the students had to sit before a group of their professors and answer questions. Like the inquisition, Edith thought. Italy had a lot to offer.

She patted her upper lip where a few drops of moisture had gathered. Here was the poem "Icescapes." She had written it after a terrific storm when she and Isabel had not been able to get out of the house because the doors froze shut. It was a poem about jealousy; Isabel had flirted outrageously with a visiting poet at a dinner the night before. The dinner, then the storm. All night they had listened to the trees cracking, branches hurtling down like ice swords, and in the morning, when they looked out the window, it was as if the world was made of glass. She would definitely read this poem, which would seem exotic to her Roman audience. Carefully she laid a strip of paper against the margin of the page and wrote the title on the list for Amelia, who would be reading the translations with her. Wouldn't the double-entendre on the word *ice-pick* get lost in translation? This seemed amusing, the idea that richness, nuance, got lost in translation. Where did it go? She imagined the land of what was lost in translation, imagined herself in it.

She was happy doing this, making these choices, browsing through this world of her own making; she felt at ease, at rest. Tonight's audience, Amelia had told her, would be larger than on the first night, and a greater proportion of it would be serious students of English who were familiar with her work. She felt the pleasant excitement she often had before a reading, hoping her delivery of the poems would be illuminating, giving her audience a sense of greater intimacy with the words on the page.

Could she do what Isabel wanted? Could she stay here and leave everything she knew behind? She looked out the window, at the dark leaves of a tree and the fresher green of a vine curling over the sill, patiently working the frame loose from the wall. There was something in it that was not a leaf. As Edith focused upon it, it moved. It was a lizard, small, bright green, with a pink throat, opening and closing over its glassy eyes the mauve double folds of its curious eyelids. It took one cautious step onto the dusty stone ledge.

Edith watched the lizard, fairly holding her breath at the strangeness of it. She had the sensation that some reliable anchor was being cut away, and she was now completely adrift. A line from a gospel song she had heard—but where? when?—ran through her confused thoughts: "Praise God, the open door. I ain't got no home in this world anymore." Where am I? she thought. She had a sharp recollection of the field outside her parents' house, a hot summer day; she was sitting on the porch, angry voices raised behind her, gnats batting against her face, the hum of insects, and before her the flat yellow expanse of the field, which had been mowed and would soon have to be hayed, a job she hated.

Isabel had said coming to Rome was like coming home, and Edith had to take her word for it, because she had not ever had that sensation in her life and she doubted she ever would. It was too late now to find a home to go back to. She pictured herself lying flat on her back on the floor of a leaky rowboat, above her face the blue sky, and all around water, water, to the end of the world. In the distance she heard a door open, which she registered unconsciously as the door of the lecture room. Then there was the sound of rapid footsteps coming toward her. The lizard heard it too, scurried across the sill, disappeared into the vine. Edith abandoned her reverie and turned from the window to see Isabel approaching, moving swiftly with the dancer's powerful, slightly duckfooted gait. She was exhausted, Edith observed. Her eyelids were still swollen from last night's tears, and there were dark circles beneath them. She'd pulled her hair back tightly and made a schoolmarmish bun at the nape. She hadn't neglected the lipstick, which was bright red, but it only served to outline the downward cast of her mouth.

The ugly business at the college had shaken Isabel, Edith

understood. She was wounded by it in some vital center of her confidence. It was her way to dismiss what she couldn't control, and put the best possible face on every failure, and that was what she was doing now, but it was hard, she was having a hard time of it. She came to the doorway and leaned against the frame, giving Edith the wan smile of a comrade in arms. "Are you ready?" she asked.

THE CHANGE

Gina had all the symptoms: sleep disturbances, hot flashes, irritability, weight gain, loss of libido, aching joints, and heart palpitations. The one she complained of most was hot flashes, which she dealt with by throwing off her clothes and cursing. As far as Evan was concerned, her irritability was the worst symptom; she was increasingly difficult to get along with. Churlish, he told her. Her lack of interest in sex was possibly more frustrating, though he admitted to himself that he found her less desirable because she was so uncivil, so he did not suffer unduly from wanting her and being rejected. When they did make love, it was a wrestling match, which Evan enjoyed well enough. They had never been much for tender embraces.

Her work was changing, too; it was getting darker. As he stood looking at an engraving of trees, of a dark forest, he wondered how it could all seem so clear when it was almost entirely black. She was working all the time, well into the nights, because she couldn't sleep. Often enough he found her in the mornings curled up under a lap rug on the cot in her cluttered, inky little studio with the windows open and the chill early morning light pouring in.

She wasn't taking care of herself properly, not eating enough, not washing enough, she hardly took any exercise at all. Sometimes she lay around the living room all day, napping or reading magazines, getting up now and then to rummage around in her studio, then back to the couch, where she left ink stains on the upholstery. There were dustballs under the beds and in the corners of the rooms, dishes always stacked in the sink.

"It's driving me crazy," Evan complained. "Can't we get someone in to clean this place, since you can't keep up with it?"

She gave him a cold, reproachful glare over her magazine. "I *can* keep up with it," she said. "I just *don't* keep up with it."

"Well, then, hire someone who will."

"You hire someone," she replied. "Since it bothers you so much."

Evan turned away. He did all the cooking as it was. How could he possibly take on the cleaning as well? And he had no idea how to hire someone. He went to the kitchen and threw open the refrigerator. "And what are we going to eat for dinner?" he shouted to her. "This refrigerator is practically empty."

"We'll go out," she shouted back.

They went out. She was in a good mood for a change. They laughed, drank too much wine, walked back through the city streets with their arms locked around each other, made love on the living room floor. Evan went to bed but she wouldn't go with him. She went to her studio, and twice when he woke in the night, he saw that the light was still on.

The next day she was a harridan again, peevish and distracted. His own work was going poorly, he had taken on too much and had two deadlines he didn't think he could make. When he complained to her, she shrugged. "Then don't make them," she said. "Tell the editor you can't do it."

"Right," he said. "And then she never calls on me again. I need the work."

"You always say that," she snapped. "And you always have more work than you can do. So, obviously you don't need it."

Evan followed her out of the room into her studio. "I don't always have more than I can do. Sometimes I don't have any. It's feast or famine in this business, as you well know."

Gina yawned, put her hands on her hips, and stretched, making an agonized face at him. "Jesus, my back hurts," she said.

"It's freezing in here," he said, moving toward the open window. "Why don't you close this?"

But before he could reach it she blocked his path. "Don't close the window," she said angrily.

"Ugh," Evan said. "What is that?" For on the windowsill were the remains of some animal. Evan pushed past his wife to get a closer look. It was the back half of a mouse, tail, feet, gory innards.

"Where did this come from?" he said.

"The cat must have left it." She turned away, bending over a partially engraved plate.

"We don't have a cat."

All at once she was angry, as if he'd done something annoying. "The neighbor's cat," she sputtered. "Would you just leave it. I'll take care of it."

"It's disgusting," he said. He looked around the room at the half-empty coffee cups, the dishes with crumbs and bits of old sandwiches or dried cottage cheese stuck to them, the confusion of ink and paper, copper plates, presses, the disorder of the bottles of acids and resins, the writing desk overflowing with unanswered mail, bills, and photographs. "This whole room is disgusting," he concluded. "How can you find anything in here?"

To which she replied, "Who asked you to come in here? Will you get out of here?" And she pushed him out the door.

*

They were invited to a dinner party. Gina was in her studio until it was almost time to leave. Then she came out, washed her hands, combed her hair, threw on a skirt, and said she was ready. Evan had showered, shaved, dressed carefully, even polished his shoes. He looked at her skeptically. "That's it?" he said. "You're ready?"

"Why not?" she said.

No jewelry, he thought. No makeup, no perfume. There had been a time when it took her at least an hour to dress for a party.

The party went well, it was easy conversation, good wine, old friends, until a couple Gina and Evan had not seen for some time arrived. Evan spotted the woman, Vicky, first, smiled and waved as he caught her eye. Something was different about her, he thought, but he couldn't be sure. She looked great, very bright, very intense. Her blouse had flecks of gold in it; she was sparkling. Gina, standing next to him, laughing at something their host was saying, turned and saw the woman, too. "Oh my God," she said softly. Vicky moved slowly toward them, smiling.

Seeing Gina's drop-jawed amazement, the host said confidentially, "She's been done." Evan sent him an inquiring look, to which he responded by tapping his lower jaw with the backs of his fingers.

Vicky had stopped to speak to someone else. Evan watched her, though he tried not to stare. In a distant, agreeable way he had always admired her. The last time he had seen her, several months ago, he had observed that her delicate beauty was fading. Now she looked good, he thought. She'd changed her hair, too, probably to disguise the more surprising change in her face. They'd done a good job on her. Perhaps her mouth was a little stretched at the corners, and of course the flesh around her chin looked tight. She broke away from her conversation and continued toward Gina and Evan.

"Vicky, how are you?" Evan said, catching her outstretched hand in his own, as if he were retrieving her, he thought, or pulling her out of a fish tank. "It's good to see you."

He was aware of Gina at his side, of her steady, even breathing, but he didn't see her face until it was too late. "Have you lost your mind?" she said sharply to Vicky. "Why would you do something like that? You look awful."

Vicky missed a beat to astonishment and another to dismay, but that was all. "I may have lost my mind," she said, "but you seem to have lost your manners."

Evan turned on his wife. He was so angry he wanted to slap her. "For God's sake, Gina," he said. "Are you drunk?"

Gina blinked her eyes rapidly, ignoring him. She was concentrated on Vicky, who was easing herself away. "So you count on people not to say anything. Do you tell yourself they don't notice?"

"Excuse me," Vicky said, disappearing into the crowd.

"It's ridiculous," Gina continued. "She looked perfectly fine before. Now she looks like something from television, like a talk-show host."

"I think we'd better go," Evan said, trying to take her arm, but she shook him off.

"Will you calm down," she said.

So they stayed and the rest of the evening passed uneventfully, but Evan was miserable and felt humiliated. At dinner they were seated as far from Vicky and her husband as possible, probably at her request, Evan thought. Vicky was the center of attention; Evan could hear her tinkling laugh, but couldn't bring himself to look her way. Gina leaned out past him now and then to shoot a disapproving look toward the offending jawline, but she said nothing more about it, and once she got into a conversation with her neighbor, which Evan joined, she seemed to forget the unpleasant incident. They talked about publishing—the neighbor was also a journalist—and then about travel. Gina told a funny story about a hotel they had stayed in on a Greek island, and Evan, though he had heard this story before, though he had actually been there when the porter threw Gina's suitcase out the window, found himself laughing as heartily as their friend. He applied himself to his wine and resolved to forgive his wife.

Evan noticed the book a few times before he actually picked it up to look at it. He'd seen it on the table in the living room, half buried in a pile of magazines, and on the kitchen table, and once on the nightstand next to their bed. A woman's book about women, he thought, about all the trials of their biology and psychology, the special wonderfulness of it all and the failure of men to comprehend any of it, though it was going on right under their noses. Women lapped this stuff up like cream, even intelligent women like Gina, which was what really made it annoying. Here was the book again, jammed between the cushions of the couch with a pencil stuck in it to mark the page. He pulled it out and opened it to the page with the pencil. The chapter was titled "No Longer a Woman," and it told all about the biological changes attendant on the menopause, the shrinking of the uterus, the drying out of vaginal tissue, the atrophy of the ovaries, the steady depletion of estrogen. Pretty dry reading, Evan thought with a sardonic chuckle. He put the book back where he had found it and wandered off to his desk, where his article was not taking shape. No longer a woman, he thought. But if not a woman, then what? It was ridiculous. When was a woman ever not a woman?

All the symptoms Gina complained of only proved she was a woman, and a susceptible one at that, which was part of being a woman, too. An old woman was still a woman, still behaved as she always had, only more so. Evan thought of his grandmother. Not an old woman but an old lady. She wore violet perfume, he could still remember it, and was fond of a certain candy, a puffy, spongy, fruit-flavored ball that came in tins; he hadn't seen any in years. She was small, bent, arthritic, but industrious to the end. She did a little gardening on the last day of her life. She had survived her husband by twenty years. Perfectly nice, perfectly sexless. Serene, agreeable. Everyone loved her.

Though he remembered that once, when he was praising this wonderful woman to his mother, she had commented drily, "Yes, she's very nice now. But she wasn't always."

Their son, Edward, called. Gina answered the phone. Evan stood by waiting for his turn; he was fond of his son and looked forward to these weekly calls. Gina was smiling. She laughed at some witticism and said, "Watch out for that." Then for several minutes she fell silent. Her eyes wandered around the room, never set-tling, and she shifted her weight from foot to foot restlessly. At last she said, distantly, "That's really great, dear. Here's your father. I'll talk to you next week," and held out the phone to Evan.

While he stood talking to Edward, Gina sat down at the table and pulled off her sweater. Then, as Edward went on about his psychology class, she stripped off her shirt and bra. She stretched her arms out across the table and rested her head upon them. Evan turned away from her and tried to concentrate on his son's description of his daily life. When he hung up the phone she was sitting up, blotting her forehead with her sweater.

"You were a little abrupt with him," Evan said. "He asked if you were OK."

"Of course I'm OK," she said.

Evan took a seat next to her and watched as she pulled her shirt back over her head. "Did he tell you about his psychology professor?"

"Yes," she said. "He talks too much."

Evan ran his hand through his thinning hair, trying to stroke down his impatience. "You're not the only one who's getting older, you know."

She pushed back her chair, dismissing him. She was on her way to her studio. "It's not the same," she said in parting. "It's different."

It was always different, he thought. They wanted to be treated the same, but only with the understanding that they deserved special treatment because they were different. It was true that they had been treated as if they were different for a long time, but they had been treated as different in the wrong way, they were not different in that way. What was different was the deal they got, the way they were treated, which was never fair. He loosened his collar; his face felt hot. But oh no, it wasn't anything that wasn't his fault. It wasn't hormones surging uncontrollably like guerrilla fighters, it was just his lousy blood pressure which was elevated by his annoyance with his wife's suffering, and if he was uncomfortable, if he felt a little snappish, well, it was all his fault, because *her* bad temper was a symptom, and *his* was just plain old garden-variety bad temper, typical in the male. He got up and staggered into his study, where his article accosted him, demanding what he could not, because of Gina, seem to give it: his undivided attention. He turned away and went into the kitchen to make coffee.

Gina had gone out to have lunch with a friend. Evan was alone in the apartment with his article. He sat at his desk reading over his notes, listening to the taped interview he had done with a teenaged girl who, he recalled, had been dressed in something that resembled two pieces of bicycle tubing. It depressed him to listen to her agitated, rage-filled monologue. She had a vocabulary of twenty-five words or so, insufficient to express any but the most basic threats and complaints. She was the current girlfriend of a gang member named Smak; Evan's article was about these girls, the attendants of brutal young men, about their precarious, angry, voluptuous, and mindless daily lives. On the tape she was trying to explain to Evan that she did not get up at the same time every day, which was why school was not a possibility for her.

He switched off the tape machine and stared at his bright computer screen for several minutes, but nothing came to him so he switched that off, too. Then he got up and wandered through the apartment to Gina's studio.

The lunch was a kind of celebration; she'd finished all the work scheduled for a show next month. There were two new engravings on the drying rack, the rest were stacked away in two big portfolios, ready to go. As Evan stood looking at one on the rack, a line from one of her catalogues ran through his head: "She is a woman who has never stopped loving the forest." They had a joke about it, a follow-up line: "And she is a woman who has never stopped living in Brooklyn."

For twenty years her subject had been the same, but this didn't mean her work had not changed. In Evan's opinion the change had been gradual and persistent. She was more patient, saw more clearly, though the prints were progressively darker. That was the odd, wonderful thing about the newer prints; though they seemed to be covered with ink they were full of an odd kind of light, an almost subterranean glow. In this one, for instance, he could see through a tangle of vegetation to the ground beneath, and on that dark ground he could make out the tracks of some small animal, a mouse or a chipmunk. In both the prints on the rack, the viewpoint was high, as if the viewer were above it all, in a tree perhaps, looking down. Evan studied the second one. He seemed to be falling into it; it was truly an exhilarating angle. There, as he looked deeper and deeper through the accumulation of lines, he made out something extraordinary. He crouched down, close to the paper. It was the small hind foot of a rabbit, no bigger than his fingernail, but perfectly clear. In the next second, he knew, it would be gone.

He went to the portfolio, opened it, looked at the first print. Again the odd feeling of vertigo seized him as he looked down upon the teeming world of branches and vines. He could almost hear the dull buzz of insect life, breathe the oxygen-laden air. "These are terrific," he said aloud. No wonder she had been so absorbed, so distracted, so uninterested in the daily course of her life. He felt a little stab of jealousy. His own work did not claim him; he had to drag himself to it. But that feeling passed quickly. He sat down on her cot, flushing with excitement, imagining how the room would look filled with his wife's strange vision. He heard her key in the door, her footsteps in the hall, then she was standing in the doorway looking in at him.

"What are you doing in here?" she said, just an edge of territorial challenge in her tone.

"I was looking at the new work," he said.

She leaned against the door frame, pushed her hair off her forehead. She'd had a few drinks at lunch, celebrating. "Well, what do you think?" she said.

"I think it's just amazing," he said. "It's so good I had to sit down here and mull it over."

She sagged a little more in the doorway, smiling now but anxious. "Do you really think so? I've been almost afraid for you to see it."

"Oh, my dear," he said.

Tears filled her eyes. She brushed them away with the back of one hand. "I'm so happy," she said. She came into the room and sat beside him, still wiping away tears. "These stupid tears," she said impatiently.

Evan put his arm around her, muttered into her shoulder, "I'm so proud of you." There they sat for some time, contented, holding on to one another as if they were actually in the forest of her dreams.

There was always a letdown after she'd finished a block of work, Evan told himself in the difficult days that followed. She was petulant and weepy, angry with the gallery owner, who had been her friend and supporter for years, complaining about every detail of the installation. She hardly slept at night, though what she did in her studio Evan couldn't figure out. She wasn't working and she hadn't, as she usually did between showings, cleaned the place up. But night after night he woke just long enough to watch her get up, pull on her robe, and go out, then he saw the light from her studio. During the day she lay about the apartment, napping or reading, getting nothing done and snapping at him if he so much as suggested a trip to the grocery. He tried to ignore her, spent his days struggling with his article, which resisted his efforts so stubbornly he sometimes sat at his desk for hours, literally pulling at what he called the remains of his hair. Finally he began to have trouble sleeping, too. He lay on his back in the darkness while panic gripped his heart, unable to move or to rest. When he did sleep, he had strange, unsettling dreams in which he was lost, pursued by something terrifying, powerful, something silent and brooding, something with wings.

One night, waking in terror from such a dream, he found himself, as he often did, alone in the bed. Once his heart slowed down and strength returned to his legs, he resolved to get up. His throat was parched, he felt dehydrated, as if he had been wandering in a desert. Pursued by what? he thought as he sat up and fumbled around for his slippers. Some desert creature? A creature with claws and wings and the face of a woman who would pose some unanswerable riddle before tearing him to bits? The idea amused him as he stumbled to the kitchen and switched on the lights, which made him recoil so violently he switched them back off. He poured himself a glass of water, and stood, still sleep-shocked, gazing out the kitchen window at the back of the building across the alley. Above it he could see the milky luminescence of the half-moon. He finished his water, feeling quiet now, and friendly. The light from Gina's studio made a pool across the kitchen floor. He put his glass in the sink and followed this light to her room. The double doors had glass insets, but the glass was mottled so as not to be transparent. They were closed, but not tightly—in fact one stood free of the latch and could be opened noiselessly with a push. He didn't want to startle her, but if she was asleep he didn't want to wake her, either. "Gina?" he said softly once, then again. Carefully he pushed the door open a few inches. He could see the cot from where he was; she wasn't in it. He opened the door a little farther, then all the way. The window stood open, the room was bright and cold; Gina was not in it.

It took him a moment to apprehend this information. He looked around anxiously, as if he could make her materialize by his determination to find her there. He went to the living room, perhaps she was sleeping on the couch; he looked in the bathroom and then the bedroom, though, of course, he knew she was not there. He glanced at the clock, three a.m. He went back to the studio.

What did it mean? How often in the past months, when he had believed her to be here in this room, had she been . . . wherever she was? His heart ached in his chest, he laid his hand upon it. She had a lover, there could be no doubt of it. That was why she was so tired all the time, why she slept all day, and why she was so cold and bitter.

Evan switched off the light and went to sit on the couch in the living room in the dark. He would wait for her; they would have it out. His rival was probably much younger than he was. When women Gina's age could, they often did. He thought of Colette and George Eliot. He would be a young man impressed by her because she was an artist and he was, surely, a nothing, a boy in need of a mother. It went like that; there were countless such stories. The minutes ticked by. He waited in a fog of anxiety and weariness. He wasn't up to the scene to come. Perhaps he should get back in bed and pretend he didn't know. Maybe then the affair would run its course, she would tire of the young man, or he of her, and things would get back to normal.

He was awakened by a clatter coming from Gina's studio. It sounded like someone was smashing china. He leaped to his feet, crossed the narrow hall, and threw open the doors. The early morning light was soft and pale, bathing the scene before him in a wash of pink and gray. Gina was on her hands and knees on the floor just inside the window. Next to her was a broken plate. A few crusts had flown from it and landed near her foot. One was lodged in the cuff of her pants.

"What on earth are you doing?" he cried.

She sat up, rubbing her ankle, picking out the bit of bread. "What does it look like I'm doing?" she said crossly. "I'm trying to get up off the floor."

"But where have you been? You weren't here."

She lifted her head toward the window. "I was on the fire escape."

She couldn't have come in the door, Evan reasoned. She would have had to walk through the living room and he would have seen her. "What were you doing out there?" he complained. "Didn't you hear me call you?"

"No," she said. "I guess I fell asleep." She got to her feet, brushing herself off. Evan pushed past her and stuck his head out the window. "How could you sleep out here?" he called back to her. In the summer she kept plants on the landing, herbs and geraniums, and on hot nights she sometimes took a cushion and sat among the pots. But now there was nothing but the cold metal, the cold air, and the cold stars fading overhead in a pale sky. The stairs led down to a narrow alleyway, which opened into a school parking lot that was fenced and locked at night. She couldn't have gone down there. His eye was caught by something on the landing below. It was a long brown feather with a black bar across it. He turned from the window to his wife, who was sitting on the cot, her head in her hands.

"You don't expect me to believe that," he said.

She raised her head and gave him a brief weary inspection, as if she were looking at an annoying insect. "I don't care what you believe," she said.

"Gina, what's happening to you?" he exclaimed. "You disappear in the middle of the night, you tell me an absurd lie nobody would believe, and then you give me your too-tired-to-care routine."

"I'm not tired," she said. "I just don't care."

"We can't go on like this," he said, in despair.

"I know it," she said.

But they did go on. What else, Evan thought, could they do? He accepted her story, partly because he couldn't come up with an alternative scenario—she had been coming in through the window, and the fire escape, as she pointed out, led nowhere—and partly because it didn't seem to matter. He didn't think she was having an affair because she didn't act like someone who was in love; she was neither defensive nor elated, and she seemed completely uninterested in her own body. What he had often thought of as a brooding sensuality now became just brooding. He continued his struggle with his article, Gina battled it out with her gallery, and finally they were both finished and both were moderately successful. They had a little time to rest, to cast about for new projects. Usually when this happened they gave themselves over to the pleasure of having no deadlines, sleeping late, eating at odd hours, gorging on videos, food, and sex. But this time it was different. Gina was still sleeping very little at night, and she seemed so uninterested in sex Evan made a resolution that he would not initiate it. In the past, he thought gloomily, he had never paid much attention to who started it. Now he was self-consciously aware that it was always him. She rejected him without speaking, with a shrug, or by walking away. And if she did accept his overtures, she hurried him along, as if she didn't really have the time and her mind was somewhere else. He grew sick of trying and sick of waiting. Winter was dragging on; the weather was rotten, cold and rainy.

Evan was drinking too much, and for the first time in his life he began to put on weight. One Sunday when the sun was shining for a change and there was a hint of warmth in the air, he ran into a neighbor at the farmers' market. During their conversation Evan jokingly mentioned the latter problem; the drinking was a secret he was keeping even from himself.

"It happens to the best of us," his neighbor said. "Especially at our age. I've joined a gym; it's not far from here. It's made a big difference in how I feel."

Evan had to admit that his neighbor looked fit and energetic. "Give me a call," the neighbor concluded. "I go two or three times a week. I'll take you over and show you around. Bring Gina, if she's interested."

But of course she wasn't interested. "It's ridiculous," she said, throwing one magazine on the floor and taking up another. "I'm not going to spend my time running on a treadmill like a laboratory rat."

So Evan went alone. He met his friend at the reception desk and received a pass, then a tour of the facility. He was impressed with the size of the place, the up-to-date equipment, swimming pool, racquetball courts—he hadn't played in years but he remembered enjoying the game—there was even a juice and salad bar. It was in this bar, as he was leaving, that he found Vicky and her husband, who waved him over to their table with soft cries of enthusiasm and surprise. As he walked to join them, Evan experienced a mild pang of discomfort; he hadn't seen either of them since Gina had behaved so rudely at the party. But Vicky seemed not to remember, or not to care. Her hand pressed his warmly in greeting and she patted the chair next her, inviting him to sit.

"So you're thinking of joining up?" her husband, Victor, inquired.

Evan smiled at him and nodded, looking around the pleasant,

busy room. He was thinking, as he always did when he saw them together, Vicky and Victor, such silly names. "It's much bigger than I thought it would be," he said.

Vicky drained her carrot juice. "We've been coming for a year now. It's a lifesaver."

"You look great," Evan said. She really did. She was wearing a sleeveless scoop-neck leotard and leggings so he could see exactly how good she looked. There was just a hint of cleavage visible at the neckline, enough to show that her breasts were still firm, not sallow-looking or wrinkled. Her arms looked firm and strong, too, though the thick cords and darkened skin on the backs of her hands gave some hint of her age. She had a scarf tied around her waist, not the best idea, Evan thought, because it called attention to the small but distinctly round belly just below. He couldn't see her hips. She pushed her hair back from her face, giving Evan a quick, complex look made up in parts of gratitude, flirtation, and suspicion. "Thanks," she said. "I feel great."

Victor patted her shoulder proprietarily. "She's fantastic," he said. Vicky laughed, childishly pleased to be the object of her husband's praise. Evan looked down at himself with fake dismay. "I'll need a lot of work," he said. "It may be too late for me."

"Never too late," Victor assured him. "You're as young as you feel."

Evan wished they could talk about something else, but there was no way to change the subject. This was a gym, after all. The subject was bodies. Victor told Evan about his routine. He liked the stair-step machine, Vicky preferred the treadmill. The aerobic classes were excellent. Vicky even did yoga. The free-weights room was sometimes a little crowded; the young jocks did not always leave the racks in perfect order, that was the only drawback. At last there was a lull long enough for Evan to make an excuse. He had to get back to work, he said. As always, he had a deadline.

"Time for us to hit the showers," Victor said, getting up. He popped Vicky playfully across the shoulders with his towel. "Great to see you," he said, grasping Evan's hand. "Give Gina our best."

Evan noted the brief flash of distress that crossed Vicky's face at the mention of his wife. She remembers perfectly well, he thought. She's just being nice about it. Then he was angry at Gina all over again. What right had she to criticize this nice woman because she cared enough about her appearance to have her face lifted? What was wrong with staying fit and wanting to look good for each other, as Vicky and Victor obviously did?

Evan left the gym with a printed sheet of membership privileges and prices gripped tightly in his hand. Filled with resolution and optimism, he stopped in the chilly parking lot to look it over. This was a good thing to do, he told himself. He wanted to be like Vicky and Victor. Gina would ridicule him but he didn't care. He wanted to feel good about himself, he wanted to change his life. Carefully he folded his informational paper and put it deep in his coat pocket.

That night Gina was particularly restless and distracted. Evan made pasta and a salad for dinner but she hardly touched it. She complained that her neck and shoulders were stiff, shrugging repeatedly, trying to loosen up the muscles. Evan told her about the gym, expecting a tirade, or simply a dismissive remark, but to his surprise she listened attentively. In fact, as he explained why he thought it would be a good investment for him, how he feared that his sedentary ways resulted in fatigue and depression, she seemed to focus on him with a distant but sincere interest. "It can't be good for you to be closed up in here with me all the time," she said.

"It's not that," he protested.

She said nothing. Evan chewed a piece of lettuce. He could feel her eyes on his face. At last he looked up at her, expecting to find contempt, or anger, or indifference, but she was studying him with a look of complete sympathy, devoid of pity or self-interest, as if, he thought, she were looking right into his soul and finding it blameless, but also infinitely sad. He felt a hot flush rising to his cheeks and he looked away, at his fork resting among the salad greens, at his half-full glass of wine.

"I think it's a good idea," she said.

They sat together on the couch watching a video. It was a complicated story of intrigue on a Greek island. Evan had chosen it because the cover showed a man standing in front of a white building set against a sky so blue and so clearly warm he wished he was in the picture. The scenery in the film was terrific; the television screen seemed to pour warmth and color into their drab living room. When it was over Evan talked a little about how much he wanted to travel, to go to Greece again, and also to Italy and Spain, warm sunny countries where the people were relaxed and friendly and the food was fresh, healthful, and prepared with care and enthusiasm. Now that their son was grown they could think about going off-season, when there were no tourists. Gina listened, inserting qualifiers here and there—the food in Spain was notoriously filthy, the Italians were far from relaxed—but she seemed more amused than irritated by his aimless fantasies. "You're full of desires today," she said.

"It's true," he admitted. "I am." He rubbed his hand along her thigh, nuzzled his face against her shoulder. She neither responded nor pushed him away. He brought his hand up to her breast, took her earlobe gently between his teeth. "Please don't," she said softly.

He dropped back on the couch, letting out a sigh of frustration.

"I'm sorry," she said, getting up.

"Don't worry about it," he said.

She went into her studio and began gathering up dishes, wadding up pieces of paper. She left the doors open and Evan could see her from where he sat. She went into the kitchen carrying plates, came back with a garbage bag. Evan looked at the clock; it was after midnight. A great time for a little light cleaning, he thought. "A little night cleaning," he called to her.

"I can't stand it anymore," she said, amiably.

"Me neither," Evan said, but softly, to himself. She didn't hear it. After a few minutes he realized he was falling asleep. He got up, pulling off his clothes as he went to bed.

The dream ended, as he had known it must, with his missing the plane. Evan woke feeling breathless. He had been running, but they kept the planes across a busy six-lane highway from the check-in. There was a fence, too, he recalled, chain-link, tall, over six feet. He rolled onto his side and looked at the clock. It was five a.m. Gina had still not come to bed. He sat up, rubbing his head, disoriented and strangely apprehensive. After a few moments he got up and made his way to the kitchen. While he stood at the sink drinking water, it dawned on him that the lights in Gina's studio were off. She must have decided to sleep in there. Usually when he found her asleep, the lights were on, the book she had been reading had slipped to the floor or lay, still open, beneath her hand. He stepped out into the hall.

The day was just beginning to dawn and there was enough gray light for him to see his way. It was, he thought, the most beautiful time of day. The air was still, the building all around him wrapped in a nearly palpable silence, yet alive with the impending and inevitable intensification of light. It was warm in the hall; the apartment was overheated and there was no way to adjust it. A blast of cool air greeted him as he reached Gina's studio. There he stood absorbing one shock after the other.

She had left both the doors and windows wide open. The room was in perfect order; down to the pencils. Some of the habitual clutter had even been stored away in boxes, which were stacked against one wall. The cot was made up neatly: Gina was not in it. Nor was she anywhere else in the room. He said her name once, turned and looked out into the living room, but of course she wasn't there, either. He crossed the orderly studio—it seemed alien yet familiar to him, like a room in a dream—to look out on the fire escape, which he found, as he expected, unoccupied. Why was this happening? he thought. Why couldn't everything just go on as it always had? He gazed up at the pale sky, down at the iron clutter of the fire escape, across the narrow ugly yard at the opposite building. He felt an ineffable sadness curling up into his consciousness like a twining plume of smoke. The building was mostly dark, no one was up yet. One narrow window had a light on, probably a bathroom light left on all night.

He had the uncanny feeling that he was being watched. An abrupt snapping sound drew his eyes up to the ledge at the top, just one story above his own.

That was when he saw the owl.

His sadness was dissipated by this wondrous sight. He leaned out the window, craning his neck to see more clearly, "Wow," he said. "An owl in Brooklyn."

A big owl, too, or so it seemed to him. He reflected that he had never actually seen an owl before, at least not at such close range.

The bird was perfectly still but its head was inclined forward, its golden eyes were focused on Evan. Then, to his astonishment, with a sudden convulsion of motion that was as soundless as it was alarming, the owl opened its wings and flew directly at him. The distance between them, some thirty yards, disappeared in a second. Evan reeled away from the window, aware only of fierce talons extended in his direction. In the next moment he stood clutching the edge of Gina's drawing table, and the owl was perched comfortably on the window ledge, not ten feet away.

His momentary terror faded, replaced by fascination and wonder. The bird was evidently not going to attack him. There was a raised metal bar along the sill, part of the fire escape, and the owl had wrapped its feet around this. He could see the talons sticking out beneath the thick brown fluff of the legs, black and long and sharp as a cat's claws. The bill, too, looked sharp and dangerous, like a hard black finger pointing down between the large golden eyes. These eyes were fixed on Evan's face with unblinking, unnerving directness. They seemed to be looking right through him, possibly at something behind him. He shifted uneasily from one foot to the other. "I'd ask you to stay," he said, "but we're fresh out of mice."

The bird opened its beak, as if to speak, then spun its head around to face the courtyard, where some tiny motion or sound, invisible or inaudible to Evan, attracted its attention. The whole maneuver was so sudden he had only an impression of having seen it, but it seemed to him the bird's head went all the way around. The eyes drilled through him again. What a disturbing thing it was to be scrutinized in this way by a creature who had, he knew, no sympathy with him. Again the owl opened its beak, but this time a sound issued forth, a high-pitched, startling scream, such as a frightened woman might make. It was so loud and sudden it made Evan step back. Then, as suddenly, the bird was silent again. "Please," Evan said. "You'll wake the neighbors." The owl, unconcerned, fell to picking at its chest feathers. Evan stepped closer, quietly, stealthily, as if the bird didn't know with each second exactly where he was. He was so close he could have reached out to touch the beautiful mottled wings, though he knew he would not dare. The owl raised its strange, otherworldly face, made a calm sidestep on the bar, dipped its head, then refocused on his face.

"Why have you come here?" Evan asked.

But the owl only stared at him and he felt foolish for speaking. With the intrusion of this portentous creature, all the tedium and anxiety of his life had fallen away. A thrill, as of discovery, passed through him, but he did not move. It was best to be still in such a presence, which surely would not stay long or ever come again.

LIMERICK
COUNTY LIBRARY

WITHDRAWN FROM STOCK